The Detour is a highly suspenseful story with twists and turns and flavored with deep faith. This read is definitely a page turner.

Elizabeth Smith
Author of Twin Strokes

The Detour is an interesting read that will keep you in suspense until the end.

Rui Ma

When the Chŭ family rescues CIA operative Luke, they uncover an historical bond between them that leads to a thrilling mix of suspense and heroism against the backdrop of the police state of North Korea. Author Stephen Hiemstra weaves in this fateful encounter and its resolution against a well-described background to display the miraculous work of God. This exciting book is perfect for a plane trip or as a break from daily responsibilities.

Hyunok Lee
Retired Economist
University of California at Davis

The Detour is a captivating and thought-provoking novel that transports readers into the heart of North Korea. With its engaging characters, compelling storyline, and exploration of social issues, this book offers a unique and immersive reading experience. I wholeheartedly endorse this novel to anyone seeking a captivating blend of suspense, romance, and introspection.

Wilson McMillan

Stephen Hiemstra, best known for his Christian non-fiction, has branched out into thriller fiction. In *The Detour*, we see the continuing story of Luke Stevens, first introduced in *Masquerade*. Luke has to fly his ex-wife's coffin from China to the U.S. It is an ill-fated trip between a typhoon and threats against his life. When his plane crashes, Luke lands in the waters off of North Korea and is rescued by a fisherman. Stephen's research on North Korea paid off in this story as Luke is welcomed by underground Christians who vow to get him home. This is fascinating story that I think you will love as much as I do.

Ann Westerman

From the first paragraph, Stephen Hiemstra's novella, *The Detour*, captures the attention of the reader and holds it securely to the end of the book. Luke Stevens, former pastor—now CIA agent, experiences God's Psalm 91 provision in the depths of the sea and his rescue orchestrated by Christians living in North Korea. Through the threats of communism, political intrigue, grief, romance, and human trafficking, Dr. Hiemstra weaves the pattern of faith in God, even in hostile environments and difficult circumstances. Remarkably, he shows the reality of persecutions of Christians in our time, a truly thought-provoking message.

Sharron Giambanco

THE DETOUR

Other Books by the Author

THE DETOUR

A Thriller by

Stephen W. Hiemstra

T2PNEUMA PUBLISHERS LLC
CENTREVILLE, VIRGINIA

THE DETOUR: A Thriller

Names: Hiemstra, Stephen W., author.Title: The detour / Stephen W. Hiemstra. Description: Centreville, VA: T2Pneuma Publishers LLC, 2023. Identifiers: LCCN: 2023909114 | ISBN: 978-1-942199-49-6 (paperback) | 978-1-942199-53-3 (Kindle) | 978-1-942199-96-0 (epub) Subjects: LCSH Intelligence officers--Fiction. | China--Fiction. | Korea (North)--Fiction. | Thrillers (Fiction) | Romance--Fiction. | Christian fiction. | BISAC FICTION / Thrillers / General | FICTION / Romance / General | FICTION / Christian / General Classification: LCC PS3608 .I54 D48 2023 | DDC 813.6--dc23

Many thanks to my editors, Diane Sheya Higgins and Sarah Hamaker. Thanks also to Jean Arnold, Esther Eng, Robert Portland, and Elizabeth Westerman who offered comments.

The cover art is called *The Good Samaritan* by He Qi (www.heqiart.com). Used with permission.

ACT ONE

2 - The Detour

Chapter One

*L*uke Stevens walked hand in-hand with Abi Ling (a.k.a. Ling Xiu) from their hotel to the Beijing Hospital to visit Harry Bai (a.k.a. Bai Cheng). *Was it really late morning and still September? Was Luke, former pastor and newly minted, CIA agent, really spending time with Abi, medical student and daughter of China's premier?* The terrorist attack just days earlier left Harry, Minister of State Security, in the hospital recovering from gunshot wounds. It left Luke in a daze, wondering what was real and what not.

Maybe it was the dazzling silk dress that Abi wore or the unusual detail expressed in her make-up, not that she needed any. Luke felt underdressed in his navy polo shirt and blue jeans. Sure, they both wore comfortable walking shoes, but Abi's soft-sole oxfords improbably matched the pink of her dress.

Dodging bicyclists and pushing through the crowds as her security team struggled to keep up, Abi stopped at a corner for the traffic light. Amid the street clatter, the smell of heated asphalt, and the sun glaring overhead, she turned and looked straight at Luke.

"Marry me!"

I haven't even yet buried my ex-wife Sarah Gomer and Abi wants to plan a wedding? Luke felt like a man caught naked coming out of a shower. Sarah Gomer died of ovarian cancer and needed now to be flown back to Northern Virginia for burial—Luke still felt numb with grief and had trouble managing daily activities, like walking unassisted. He caught his breath as he stopped to absorb Abi's proposal surrounded by curious onlookers.

"You're serious? This is not one of those photos-in-a-wedding-gown-fetish things?" He puzzled briefly. "Yes, absolutely, I love you and would like nothing better than to spend the rest of my life with you." Luke was not used to being led; much less being rushed into intimate conversations. Women in the crowd who had been listening surreptitiously to their conversation as they walked began to clap, recognizing Abi, seeing Luke's facial expressions, and implicitly understanding what had just been said. "Did you have a time and place in mind for the wedding?"

As the light turned green, Abi began tugging him down the street, followed by numerous onlookers. "How about over Christmas break at your church in Virginia? My family will come. It will be convenient for your family and friends. We can even invite the vice president."

Abi's security team looked worried and called for backup on their cell phones. What started out as a walk across town started to feel like a parade with people pushing and shoving to get a closer look at them.

What would Harry say about this crowd? "Do you think that is enough advanced notice to attract such a high-powered group or to find a suitable wedding dress?" Luke asked, pretending to be oblivious to the crowd. *Who proposes in front of a crowd on a city street corner?*

"Of course, silly. For us, everyone will clear their calendars. It will be fun. I'll hire a wedding planner to take care of all the details. Wedding dresses are much easier here in Beijing than in Washington."

Boy, would I hate being that wedding planner or dressmaker! "Super. Most brides go into meltdown at this point, but it sounds like you have it all thought out," Luke concluded. "If we are to be married in December, we need to get you a ring. Remember that I must fly Sarah back tomorrow evening to McLean for a funeral."

A news van pulled up. A television crew hopped out and began filming the couple and their followers, perhaps tipped off by an unscrupulous member of the security team.

"I know just the place. Beijing's finest jeweler is just around the corner across from the hospital." Abi smiled and waved at the camera like the Queen of England as she led him by the hand through the crowd to the jewelry store.

Am I really worthy of love and all this attention? What have I signed up for here? Luke thought as he rushed along, but all he said was: "Does this jeweler accept credit cards?"

§

Twenty-five-year old Chǔ Yong Dae, who wore a white, button-up blouse with a black-pencil skirt, fast-walked from her dorm room at Kim Il-Sung University in Pyongyang, the Democratic People's Republic of Korea (a.k.a. North Korea) to the school law library. She had been there many times, but this time she needed to consult the rare book collection that was isolated on the third floor for a class assignment on the country's constitution. Access to the collection was restricted because many of these books were fragile, smelled of mildew, and were banned by the Communist Party. The guard at the door checked her identification and verified from his list that Yong Dae had been granted permission to view the collection.

Entering the room, Yong Dae noticed a glass case against the far wall containing only one black leather Bible and a porcelain figurine of an American waterfowl. A brass plate read: Gift from Billy Graham to Kim Il-sung, 1992. Curious, she bowed and asked the librarian, "Who is Billy Graham?"

"He was an American pastor whose wife, Ruth, studied in a Pyeng Yang Foreign School in the 1930s when the Pyongyang was still held captive to foreign capitalist missions. Her school was destroyed by bombing during the war, but Graham visited the site anyway. He gave a lecture at the university at the invitation of Supreme Leader Kim Il-Sung," the librarian said.

Yong Dae smiled and thought to herself, *I really like the name, Ruth.*

The display seemed out of place. "Why is there a Bible in the law school library? Isn't it illegal to own a Bible?" Yong Dae said.

"Some scholars believe that the Great Leader got the idea for his Ten-Point Principles from reading the Bible's discussion of the Ten Commandments. Of course, we aren't supposed to talk about that," she whispered. "Anyhow, it must have been a different Bible because his principles were first published in 1974, almost twenty years before Mr. Graham's visit."

"Did you attend this lecture by Pastor Graham?" Yong Dae asked, hoping that the librarian would reveal more of herself.

"No, but it changed my life."

Yong Dae intuited that the librarian was too young to have attended a lecture in 1992.

"How so?"

"Mr. Graham's lecture focused on the importance of religion in American life and politics. I was surprised and curious to learn more, which I did later." The librarian smiled and said no more, but it was clear what she meant.

"Does the library have a video or audio tape of the Graham lecture?" Yong Dae asked, confident that she knew the answer to this question.

"Yes. There is an audio tape, but it is in English. I have listened to the tape so many times that I have practically memorized it and feel like I attended the lecture. I have heard that there are bootleg copies of this tape floating around, but who can say if it is true?"

Yong Dae smiled. "Can you recommend a good book on the North Korean constitution, not written by Kim Il-Sung?"

Kim Il-Sung became the founder and Supreme Leader of North Korea in 1948 to rule until his death in 1994. His son, Kim Jong-Il, rose to power after him, ruling from 1994 until 2011. After that, his son, Kim Jong-Un, rose to power and continues to rule as Supreme

Leader.

§

At the hospital, Luke asked at the information desk for directions to Harry's room and a volunteer escorted them to it. Harry's room had a private interior room with armed guards posted outside his door. Abi waved her ID at the guards and walked in still holding Luke's hand. Harry sat in bed wearing a white hospital gown and eating fresh fruit, scrambled eggs, and toast for breakfast.

Bouquets of red, white, and yellow roses—the colors of the Chinese national flag—sweetened an otherwise dull room along with photographs of his family and a few potted ferns and bamboo. Conspicuously displayed next to these were an Olympic gold medal and a photograph of Harry in a karate gi with a Harvard banner in the background. Bach's *Toccata and Fugue in D Minor* for organ played lightly in the room.

"How is our hero patient?" Luke asked, pulling up chairs, and inviting Abi to sit.

"Thankful for new and improved body armor.

Still, I would be dead if the bullet that hit me had not first bounced off of the van door. Body armor can't stop a direct hit from an AK-47 round. As it is, I'm recovering from a couple of broken ribs. It's like someone hit me with a baseball bat," Harry said patting his chest.

"Thank God you're still with us." Abi smiled, like someone hoping you'd guess it's their birthday.

"How are you two doing?"

Abi held up a bent wrist to show Harry her ring and her face beamed. "We're engaged." Luke toyed with the receipt from the jewelry store in his pocket.

"We plan a wedding in December at my church in McLean. You are the first person that we have told," Luke piped in. "I hope that you will join us."

"Count on it," Harry said. "You probably don't yet know that Lei Han is alive, but his near-death experience in the shoot-out left him with spells of shaking and vomiting. While in custody, he required heavy medication for anxiety and received counseling. He later escaped and is believed to have taken refuge in North Korea."

Abi gasped, visibly shaken, glancing left and right

like someone searching for an exit.

Luke turned to see what was going on. "What's wrong?"

"Lei Han and I dated in high school. He thought that he owned me and he had a bad temper for a teenager. It got so bad that I broke off our relationship." Abi paused. "He never accepted our breakup and I have occasionally caught him stalking me."

Harry sat up straight, tense and alarmed. Catching himself, he relaxed like a balloon whose air had been let out and changed the subject. "I used to be tempestuous like Lei Han."

From the disconnect between his body language and comment, Luke sensed Harry's distress. "I have trouble imagining you as impulsive," Luke said. "What happened? You have always been the adult in the room."

"When I was a student at Harvard University, the Premier introduced me to my wife, who took me to church on Sundays in Boston. We attended together for several years and, after that, we married and I was never the same," Harry said. "Abi, why didn't you tell me about your relationship with Lei Han?"

Abi slumped in her chair and sheepishly responded, "I was too embarrassed."

Sensing an awkward moment, Luke stood and looked at his watch. "It is getting late. Harry, I hope that you are feeling better."

Abi and Luke said their goodbyes and returned to the hotel for lunch, where Luke found a message from his boss, Tom Roberts, requesting a meeting over coffee at the U.S. Embassy at three p.m.

§

After the embassy car picked up Luke for his appointment, Abi disguised herself as a hotel worker and walked out the service entrance, carrying a plastic bag containing a change of clothes to elude her security detail. After walking a block, she slipped into a restaurant and changed clothes in the restroom. Dressed now in a white silk dress with matching shoes and purse, she walked downtown to an upscale tea shop where she found Lei Han sitting at his usual table hiding in plain view of the authorities, like a prince in exile. The fragrance of exotic teas, the black wooden paneling, and light airs of traditional Chinese string music hinted at a long history of royal patronage, including waiters who looked like bouncers in an opium den dressed up as palace guards.

"To what do I owe this great honor?" Lei Han smiled and chuckled as he stroked a Russian blue cat. He wore a grey silk dinner-jacket. His wrist conspicuously displayed a gold Rolex. The cat sported a matching gold-studded collar.

It's always about you, eh Lei Han? Abi thought. "Actually, I missed your cat. Is that the same blue, Mr. Party Chief, that I used to know and love?"

"No. No. This is Mr. Premier. Mr. Party Chief fathered a litter and I got my pick as compensation. Mr. Party Chief later passed away." Lei Han sipped his tea. "How come you avoided my question?"

Always in control, as usual. "If I recall correctly, the tea ritual requires a few minutes of polite preliminaries before any real business can commence. What exactly is this tea that you're drinking?"

"Very good—you do remember. How rude of me

to press on. This is our house surprise blend. The idea is to guess the blend based on the aroma, color, and flavor. Your order is free if you succeed. Of course, the only free order ever earned was given to a Japanese tea-shop owner who stopped by several years back," Lei Han said as he shaved a small cinnamon stick into a small teapot with a knife.

"Cute—You know that my knowledge of teas isn't up to that challenge. Okay, Lei. Let me be direct. I'm getting married." Abi held up a bent wrist to display her ring. "I need you to respect my decision and stop interfering in my personal affairs."

The cat jumped on the table, arched its back, raised a paw, and hissed loudly. "What? Who? You know I love you and you love me too, though you refuse to admit it. How can you marry someone else?" Lei Han looked down at the table and pouted.

Here we go again. "Lei, our relationship was over years ago. Neither my father nor the Chinese people would ever accept the premier's daughter marrying a Korean. Why can't you accept the truth?" Abi said.

"You're not telling the whole truth. Your father believes that my father's tea business is a front for the Triad opium trade and that he bought my mother's citizenship through the black market, forever dishonoring my family. Admit it," Lei Han said, shaking and holding back tears.

"I can't admit something I know isn't true," Abi said, knowing that Lei Han was right, but she didn't want to embarrass him further.

"So you have decided to marry that American, Luke Stevens, who rescued you in Baltimore, to further your father's ambitions? That can never be. For him, you can only be a *gumiho*—a shapesifting vixen only interested in eating his liver."

"Yes. Get over it."

"I may move on, but friends of mine won't. This detente, rapproachment, between China and the United States that your father is promoting is bad for business and your attempts to symbolize that detente in a marriage with Luke will fail." Lei Han looked up as his face tightened, no longer shaking; no longer showing weakness.

"This is confusing. Lei, what are you talking about? I'm not my father's alter-ego." Abi pretended not to understand the politics of her action.

"That's where you're wrong. In spite of your gymnastic prowess, in spite of your scholastic brilliance, in spite of all the things that make you you, till your dying breath, you're daddy's little girl, the one standing behind him in every semi-official photograph for the media. Family honor has always been your preoccupation. I'm surprised that you even took a western name in your American studies. It is my curse to love you."

"No way. You don't know me. Get over it." Abi sensed that her stridence contradicted her message and betrayed deeper, unwanted feelings.

"You're missing the big picture here. Arms manufacturers here and in the United States see peace as a threat to their livelihood. My old boss at State Security, who promoted the failed coup d'état, was just a pawn in the game of Go that these people play—they haven't gone away. The peace buzz that your engagement to the American will create will infuriate them. My rage is mostly bluster; these guys go for blood and they will come after you."

Bluster? You have already got blood on your hands.
"Lei, you're nuts. You wouldn't know a modern woman if you saw one. I'm out of here." Abi stood up and pushed back her chair to leave.

Lei Han shouted, "Don't do it!" He stood up, tipped over his chair, and knocked over a teacup. Startled, Mr. Premier ran off.

Abi eyed Lei like a seasoned black belt stepping onto the mat and backed away from his table with eyes locked. Lei stood wide-eyed, frozen, clutching his chest, like an old man on the verge of a heart-attack. The waiter-bouncers looked at Lei Han in distress, but he waived them off. Abi flung open the teashop door and marched out.

After stomping a couple of blocks, the energy flowed out of her and she winced at her own audacity. *Why did I really come here? Will Lei ever stop pursuing me as he did in the attempted abduction in Baltimore and the attack in Beijing?*

§

As the embassy car drove through Beijing, Luke found himself lost in the spacious gardens, captivating architecture, and cool fountains. *Had Marco Polo also been seduced by these same tranquil waters, unfathomable to Westerners only interested in China's spices, silks, gunpowder, and printing presses? Have I likewise been seduced or have I only breathed too deeply of the ever-present, head-spinning smog?* Never knowing who will show up at an embassy meeting, Luke wore khaki pants, a white shirt and tie, and a blue blazer, following Tom's lead.

Luke asked the driver, "Can you drop me off here? I would like to walk to the embassy."

"Sorry, sir. My orders are to escort you safely to the embassy," the driver said. "You're a person of interest, which here in Beijing can be a problem."

The car drove on to the compound and let Luke off at the front door of the main complex. A Marine guard checked his ID and escorted him to a temporary office, where Tom looked up from his computer screen as Luke walked in. Papers in English, Spanish, and Mandarin were scattered across his desk. The biggest pile was weighed down with a lighter resembling an authentic-looking M67 hand grenade.

"Come on in. How is your week shaping up?"

"I'm engaged!" Luke smiled. "On our way over to the hospital to visit Harry this morning, Abi proposed marriage and I accepted. If the sun shines on, the wind doesn't blow, and the clock keeps ticking, we plan a Christmas wedding in McLean. I hope that you will join us."

"Of course. Congratulations. You must be excited."

"I have not had time to absorb all this. I feel like a wind-blown kite being chased by a hurricane."

"It does seem a bit sudden." Tom stood up, holding out his hand. Luke reached over and shook it, pressing tight.

Luke pointed to the papers on the desk. "Are you fluent in both Spanish and Mandarin?"

"Actually, I am. I grew up in Ceiba, Puerto Rico,

when my dad was stationed at Roosevelt Roads Naval Station, but my mother hails from Hong Kong."

"You always came across as more intellectual than the typical field agent." Luke paused. "Let me switch gears a bit. Harry told us that Lei Han survived the earlier shooting and escaped custody." Luke scratched his ear. "Should I be worried?"

Tom held his finger over his lips to caution silence, closed the door, and motioned for Luke to take a seat. "Lei Han is the tip of the iceberg. He apparently was a go-between not only with Chinese State Security and North Korean intelligence services, but also between U.S. arms manufacturers at home and abroad. If his securocrat connections weren't enough, his Triad connections scare most seasoned DEA agents."

"There's more. Abi has had a personal relationship with him going back to high school, but he refused to acknowledge their later breakup. She believes that Lei continues to stalk her," Luke said.

"In other words, Lei Han has both personal and political reasons to make your life difficult and has probably been behind our troubles both in Baltimore and Beijing. We're talking a DEFCON 2 situation."

Luke stood. "I suspected as much, but let's get that coffee. I have another issue to go over with you."

§

Luke walked with Tom down to the embassy cafeteria, where the aroma of brewing espresso beckoned. Being the middle of the afternoon, their footsteps echoed through the room. The coffee concession attendant looked happy to see them. "*Hola senior Tom. Quire su cafécita de hoy?*" She prepared two espressos and gave them each a free muffin along with their coffee order. They picked a table and sat down.

"Tom, you know I am flying Sarah's coffin back to the states tomorrow evening. Even though she divorced me several years back, it seems awkward planning a wedding even before she is put to rest. I still have flashbacks of her passing out at the reception last week, her death on the way to the hospital, and the shootout that happened minutes later."

"I can imagine. How can I help?"

"With all the excitement here in Beijing I neglected to follow up on a promise that I made to Pastor Chǔ back in Northern Virginia. He helped me translate a blood-stained, leather Bible with inscriptions on the inner cover in Korean and Chinese that my father acquired during the Korean War."

Luke continued. "Pastor Chǔ explained that the first inscription is in Mandarin, written by Communist Chairman Mao Zedong to his favorite nephew, a Chinese captain and intelligence officer. The inscription instructs the nephew to inquire about how to gain the blessing of Psalm 91 for Chinese troops. The second inscription is in Korean congratulating the captain on his baptism. It was written in Pastor Chǔ's father's handwriting and signed with his initials. The Bible is dated November 26, 1950, and references Jangjin Lake, Korea, which U.S. forces called Chosin Reservoir."

"Pastor Chǔ escaped North Korea when his mother—pregnant with him—followed U.S. troops south and survived the war working as a military cook and later immigrated to the United States. My father met his father while a prisoner of war in Chinese custody. My father escaped in an informal prisoner exchange, but Pastor Chŭ's father remained behind. On reading the inscriptions, Pastor Chŭ became convinced that his father may have survived the war. When we last talked, I promised Pastor Chŭ that I would inquire about his father in Beijing, but I never followed up. Can you make some inquiries on my behalf?" Luke said.

"I'll do my best. Questions about Koreans during the war are particularly difficult to resolve. We almost never locate the people sought because many of those who survived the war ended up in North Korea. Even among those who survived the war, many were interned in prison camps or simply starved to death, a problem that remains a North Korean reality. I can tell you one thing: If those inscriptions are authentic, we're talking about some high-value intelligence, because it points to aspects of Mao Zedong's character that would likely be suppressed by hardline Marxists. Where's that Bible now?"

"The last time I saw it, it was sitting on my nightstand at my home in McLean."

"I'll make inquiries and try to secure that Bible. Your house has been kept pretty much as you left it."

Luke stood up to leave. "Tom, thanks for your help. If I don't see you before you return to Langley, have a safe trip home."

After leaving the U.S. embassy, Luke pondered his father's comments about the Korean War.

Before the Battle of Chosin Reservoir, U.S. forces went from victory to victory against Communist Korean forces and pushed them to the border with China. At that point, China intervened to support the Korean Communists. Chinese troops cut off U.S. forces from resupplying and pounded U.S. troops from mountain strongholds as they retreated along narrow valley roads below. The U.S. military remembers the Battle of Chosin Reservoir as a painful defeat and it marked a turning point in the war.

Luke's dad sometimes referred to the Korean War as the Forgotten War. North Koreans remember the war as if it were yesterday because in an attempt to turn the war around after Battle of Chosin Reservoir, the U.S. Air

Force initiated a relentless bombing campaign that leveled almost all standing structures in North Korea. The vividness of these memories is an important reason why the North Koreans government continues to invest heavily in its military and exotic weapons systems in spite of the country's desperate poverty.

Chapter Two

*A*t nine o'clock Tuesday morning, an embassy car pulled up to the Beijing Hotel with Alex (a.k.a. Major Alyssa Sunday) riding shotgun and wearing a blue pants-suit with a white blouse. As Luke walked up, Alex moved to the rear seat and Luke sat next to her dressed blue jeans, a navy polo, and a sports jacket. Luke could see in the rear-view mirror that the Chinese driver was surprised by the new seating arrangement. He was not accustomed to seeing a white guy socializing with a black woman.

Luke leaned over with his hands covering his eyes. "Alex, thank you for helping me arrange to fly Sarah home. This is an emotional journey and I am grateful for your company. Even though Sarah divorced me two years ago, I am still having trouble letting her go." He sat up and took Alex's hand. "I may need to schedule a session with the counselor."

"Not to worry, young man. You gave me an excuse to skip all those wonderful embassy briefings. We can talk any time." Alex chuckled as if she had been told an inside joke.

"Do you ever feel like the Prophet Job as Satan toyed with his life when he lost his family, possessions, and even his daily work?" Luke said. "In a single day in Baltimore, I lost my son and my own identity to terrorists in this crazy masquerade. Now, Sarah is gone and I find myself on the other side of the world living out my murdered son's life, unable even to grieve openly over her death. Tell me, am I wrong?"

"Luke, you're wrong because God is in control and you're his faithful servant. Life has a happy ending because Satan lost on the cross. The future is in Christ and he knows it, which is why he behaves so cruelly. Turn to God in your pain, center your life on Him, and deprive Satan of his de-centering sport."

"Amen. Thank you." After a few deep breaths, Luke whispered, "Let me change the subject. Did you hear whether they finished the embalming? The last time I heard, the timing would be tight."

"All done. We only need to pick out a coffin, sign a few papers, and pay the bills. The funeral home will load the coffin on the plane this afternoon, clear customs, and transport her all the way back to the funeral home in Virginia. Because Sarah identified as Muslim, the Chinese did not require cremation."

"Thank goodness."

"Remember. If you have questions about Sarah on the flight, refer to her as HR, the code word for human remains used by airlines to avoid distressing or embarrassing other passengers."

Luke looked at coffins with Alex for an hour before settling on a suitable teak coffin, a variety of wood unavailable the states. Alex signed the death certificate as the attending physician. After Sarah was placed in the coffin, Luke took photographs of her to send to relatives, said his goodbyes, and handed over a cashier's check from the Beijing branch of a U.S. bank. They then returned to the car.

"Tom told me that Abi proposed marriage and you have a Christmas wedding planned at your church in McLean," Alex said. "Oh, goodness. That was quick. Are you ready for this?"

"I did not know how best to tell you," Luke said. "I am not sure that I am ready, but I couldn't be happier."

"You, of all people, should know that it is a bad idea to make important decisions when grieving."

"Yes. You are right. Making major decisions when in grief is a rookie mistake." Luke paused. "But I am afraid that I will be stuck without a chair when the music stops—Abi makes me feel young again and helps me cope with Sarah's rejection."

"Fear is a poisonous aphrodisiac."

Luke stared off into space. Catching himself, he broke out of the trance and whispered, "Still, I hope that you will join us."

Alex leaned over to get his attention. "So you want me to be the fly in the ointment again?"

The sudden appearance of Alex's angry-black persona caught Luke off guard. *Is it repressed hostility towards Sarah for sabotaging Alex's engagement to our son years ago? Why am I the only one who triggers this reaction?*

Luke smiled. "Alex, you are no fly-in-the-ointment to people in that church. They see you as an authentic action-hero after you wrestled a bomb-trigger out of the hands of a terrorist and saved their lives only a couple weeks ago. Just put on your uniform and, this time—Major Alyssa Sunday—please wear your sword! Also, I would consider it a personal favor if you bring your son, Philip, and your mom! I want to meet them."

"Okay, okay, young man." Alex retreated into her professional persona. "Before I forget, you're flying back to Northern Virginia unescorted. Are you okay with that? Tom told me that Lei Han escaped serious injury during the shootout last week and later mysteriously eluded his guards. With him running around free, you could become a target."

"I hadn't given it a thought. Are you volunteering to serve as my bodyguard on the flight home?"

"Nope. I just hope that you'll be vigilant about security. As far as anyone on the plane is concerned, you're just another John Doe escorting HR back to a final resting place in Virginia. I suspect, however, that you'll miss the five-star food service on Air Force One. If something goes wrong, you had the agency tracking chip injected back in Virginia, so we'll always know where you are."

"Right. My scalp still itches above the right ear."

The car pulled up into the driveway in front of the Beijing Hotel.

Alex turned to Luke. "See you back in DC on Monday." She kissed him on the cheek.

"Thanks again."

Luke hugged Alex and got out of the car. As he walked away, he looked back over his shoulder and wondered how long it would be before they met again.

§

In the hotel room where Luke was a guest in her family's suite, Abi met him at the door with a hug, then handed him a glass of iced tea. Waiting on the kitchen table were sandwiches and a salad. As they sat down to lunch, an anxious look came over her face. "I'm worried about your flight. The forecast calls for a typhoon to pass over the Korean Peninsula into the Sea of Japan this evening."

"Don't worry so much. My plane will pass through the area before the storm gets there, flying too high to be disturbed much by advancing turbulence."

"Perhaps," Abi said tearing up, "but I'm still worried."

Luke held up one hand, motioning Abi to stop. "You are too anxious. Just pray that the weather does not mess with my dinner and movie," Luke smiled.

"Okay. Okay. What time do you need to be at the airport?" Abi wiped her eyes with her hand.

"I asked to observe Sarah's coffin being loaded on the plane so the funeral home advised me to be on hand a three p.m."

"I'll request a car to pick us up at two-fifteen p.m."

"Excellent." Luke paused. "Do you have some plastic wrap for my cell-phone? The battery casing protects it from regular damage and the phone itself is IP68 water resistant. Call me a germaphobe, but I would like to wrap it up to keep it clean as it goes through airport security."

"No problem."

At two-fifteen p.m., an official Chinese government car picked them up at the hotel to drive them to the airport. Luke fidgeted so much that Abi held his hand to calm him down. At the airport, a guard waived the car through the entrance to the tarmac and Luke observed through the car window Sarah's coffin being loaded on the plane. Once the coffin was loaded, the car dropped Luke off at the security gate entrance, where he saw a crowd of passengers. Abi kissed him and he went through the security gate along with all the others standing in line with their IDs and tickets in hand.

Once on the plane, the stewardess directed Luke to the second floor for the first-class section. There he sat down in his seat, which was a window seat overlooking the right wing in front of the toilet. He stowed his suitcase in the overhead bin, pulled a copy of C.S. Lewis' book, *Miracles*, out of his flight bag, and sat down. Luke's only thought was: *I really hate these long, trans-pacific flights.*

§

The head stewardess introduced the flight as offering service from Beijing to Washington Dulles airport with a refueling stop in Anchorage, Alaska. After the cabin crew gave the usual safety demonstration for a Boeing 747-8, the plane took off on schedule at four p.m. Once airborne, the captain turned off the fasten seat belt sign. Anxious about safety because of Abi's earlier angst about the flight, Luke surveyed the cabin for exits and noticed a Chinese student wearing a George Washington University tee-shirt sitting in the seat across the aisle.

Luke reached over to shake his hand. "Hi. My name is Luke."

"I'm Jake. I see that you're reading C.S. Lewis. Are you a pastor?"

"Actually, I am. Why do you ask?"

"Christian friends of mine often read C.S. Lewis quietly on the advice of their pastors. You look too old to be a student and too friendly to be a random passenger so I just figured that you must be a pastor."

"Quietly?"

"Yes. Reading C.S. Lewis in Mandarin makes it too obvious that you're a Christian so Chinese students read *Mere Christianity* in English, which most people cannot read. If anyone asks, they just say that they are practicing their English to avoid being put on a government watch-list."

"Have you read it?"

"No. I never had the guts, but I was curious about it."

"Do you know where the book came from?"

"No. Not really. Where?"

"C.S. Lewis was asked to do a radio broadcast during WWII, C.S. Lewis was asked to do a radio broadcast on the basics of Christian faith to British soldiers fighting in Europe. This theme was well received because soldiers know better than most how fragile and temporary life can be—salvation is something best not delayed. The broadcasts were so popular that after the war Lewis transcribed them into a book."

Jake whispered to Luke, "What does it mean to be saved?"

"If you pray to God for the forgiveness of your sins through Jesus Christ and ask the Holy Spirit to come into your heart to guide you, you will be saved and receive eternal life. Once you do this, you should join other Christians in walking in the faith, be baptized, and confirmed as a member of a church."

"Can you help me pray?"

"Absolutely. Repeat after me…"

Luke and Jake prayed and talked. The stewardess brought dinner, but the food trays just sat there untouched. Even as the stewardess offered headsets for a movie, Jake and Luke ignored the hustle and bustle of the cabin around them as they pursued their discussions, as if heaven and earth hung in the balance.

§

Around six-thirty, the captain came on the loudspeaker and called attention to the fasten-seat-belt sign, which had been turned on. "We have just passed over the Korean Peninsula and are flying over the Sea of Japan, which the Koreas refer to as the East Sea. Below us, if you look out the window, you can see the clouds that are harbingers of a typhoon. We're well above the storm, but we may experience a bit of turbulence."

After the captain finished speaking, Luke heard

two large explosions, one on the right and the other on the left side of the plane. The cabin lights went out, leaving only the emergency footlights around the aisles visible. Oxygen masks dropped from the compartment above, swinging back and forth as the plane shook violently and nosed down as it lost altitude. Looking out the window, Luke saw that the right engine was missing and the wing was on fire. In the dark, passengers screamed and prayed in a dozen languages.

"This is an emergency. Mayday, mayday. Flight 1250 bound for Washington Dulles is experiencing catastrophic engine failure over the Sea of Japan at 40,000 feet. Repeat. This is an emergency. Mayday, mayday. Flight 1250 bound for Washington Dulles experiencing catastrophic engine failure over the Sea of Japan."

Luke realized that in the chaos, the captain forgot to turn off the intercom, so everyone heard his mayday plea.

Luke struggled to catch his oxygen mask and put it on. The rate of descent of the plane increased. Food trays and other items bounced around the dark cabin in the turbulence. The screaming and praying continued.

"Flight 1250, this is Tokyo tower. What is your status?"

"Tokyo tower, this is flight 1250. Be advised, we're at 1,000 feet and descending rapidly. A water landing is imminent. We request immediate emergency assistance."

The captain cursed. "Attention passengers. Life jackets are under your seat. Brace for a sea landing."

Luke reached down, pulled out his life jacket, and looped it over his head. He unclipped his seat belt to place the life jacket strap around his back and attached the strap with a click.

Just before impact, the pilot raised the nose of the plane, which allowed the plane to land tail first in the water. As the plane slowed the left wing clipped a wave, throwing the plane into a spin. The fuselage split and threw Luke into the raging sea.

Luke's oxygen mask snapped off and his waist stung where his seat belt had whipped by as he was ejected. Frigid water surrounded him. He screamed and swallowed salt water. Gaining his composure, he realized that he was wearing a life jacket and felt around for the floatation cord. Finding one, he pulled it. The handle broke off. Finding another, he pulled it and felt the jacket inflating. It lifted him to the ocean's surface where he could breathe again.

Luke thanked God for his deliverance. He prayed for Jake and his fellow passengers. When the wave he was riding crested, in spite of the wind and rain he could see a slick of burning jet fuel off in the distance. No plane or people were visible, but he could smell burning jet fuel and plastic. Luke struggled to see more but the rise and fall of the waves distracted him. As time went by, the cold sea water sapped his strength and he passed out.

§

Around eight p.m. Tom was eating a late dinner alone in the hotel restaurant when he received a phone call on the cell phone that Harry had given him.

"Hello, Harry?"

"I've got bad news. Luke's plane went down in the Sea of Japan. No survivors have been reported and none are expected on account of the typhoon moving through the area."

"What?" Tom shouted. "What happened? Why don't you think that there are survivors?"

"About an hour and a half ago, the Tokyo control tower heard a distress call from the pilot who reported catastrophic engine failure—both engines—as the plane reached cruising altitude. A water landing was attempted, but the plane broke up and sank like a rock. If that weren't bad enough, the typhoon precludes rescue operations until mid-day tomorrow because of heavy wind and high seas. A Russian naval vessel passing through the area reported seeing burning jet fuel but no plane or personnel and was unable to intervene as would normally be the custom."

"How can I help?" Tom whispered, not knowing what to say.

"Any official U.S. help that can be offered in rescue and salvage operations would be appreciated."

"You've got it. Thanks for the heads up. I'll pass on the request. Have you told Abi?"

"That is my next call."

§

As Luke floated unconscious in the Sea of Japan, he found himself standing at the foot of a mountain covered with smoke that concealed a light as bright as the sun. The smoke smelled of incense and his body glowed. He felt relaxed and warmed, sheltered at odds with the typhoon raging around him. There were no winds, no waves, no sea foaming in the darkness, it was as if he were wrapped in the hands of a mighty angel.

"Am I dead?" Luke pondered.

"Thus says the LORD, he who created you, O Jacob, he who formed you, O Israel: Fear not, for I have redeemed you; I have called you by name, you are mine. When you pass through the waters, I will be with you; and through the rivers, they shall not overwhelm you; when you walk through fire you shall not be burned, and the flame shall not consume you. For I am the LORD your God, the Holy One of Israel, your Savior. I give Egypt as your ransom, Cush and Seba in exchange for you."

Luke teared up, eyes lifted to heaven. "Why me, Lord? Why me? What about the others?" The voice continued citing Isaiah 43.

"Because you are precious in my eyes and honored, and I love you, I give men in return for you, peoples in exchange for your life."

A great peace came over Luke.

§

As the vision departed, Luke heard his dead, ex-wife's voice, "Wake up, you fool!"

"Sarah? You're dead. What are you doing here? The dead are not supposed to speak to the living."

"You were supposed to be flying me home. Why can't you do anything right?"

"Calm down. I am not God. Can I help it if my plane develops engine trouble?"

"Get over it. The plane and my coffin are at the bottom of the sea. It's not fair."

"What's not fair?"

"You're alive and I'm not."

"While we are talking about what's fair, why did you divorce me and run off with that woman?"

"I don't want to talk about it."

"Then, why are you here?"

"Wake up, you fool!"

Luke opened his eyes and realized he was still floating in the sea. He wondered, *Why does Sarah still haunt me?*

§

At dawn on Wednesday morning, one hundred miles northwest of the Yamato bank in the East Sea, Captain Chǔ, piloted his forty-five-foot boat with a cargo of squid back towards Najin, North Korea, dressed in a dark-green, hooded slicker, black jeans, and brown, canvas-topped, rubber shoes. They were briefly in the eye of the typhoon that passed during the night, but the far side of the storm blowing torrential rain approached on the horizon. Thirty-foot waves continued to batter the old boat even as the sun peaked through the clouds. The storm had destroyed all drinking water and food on board, and two crew members were swept overboard. Chǔ and his two sons hung on tired, hungry, and sick.

"Father, look off starboard about a hundred meters ahead. There is a man in the water," the oldest son said in Korean.

"I see him." Chŭ steered towards the body. "It looks like a Westerner with a life-jacket, resembling those used on commercial planes."

The boat bobbed up and down in the waves as it grew closer to the body.

"Tie a rope around your brother. See if the two of you can hoist this guy on board."

One son reached over the side with a gaff hook and snagged Luke's jacket, while the other reached over the side and grabbed hold of him, pulling him on board as the boat dipped into a wave. The cold sea water soaked them and left no warmth as they sat shivering.

"Is he alive?" Chŭ asked, as his sons gasped for breath in their exhaustion and rested with the man on the deck.

"Alive, but stone-cold, shaking, and mumbling incoherently."

"Take him below. See if you can dry him off and warm him up. Put him in my bunk. If he has any identification papers or a cell phone, hide them under the ballast. If anyone asks, we know nothing about him."

Captain Chǔ returned to piloting his boat.

§

At nine o'clock Wednesday morning, Tom checked into the communications room at the U.S. Embassy in Beijing.

"I need a secure line to the operations room at CIA Headquarters in Langley," Tom requested of the officer on duty.

"Sir, step into the communications room and shut the door," the duty officer replied.

Tom entered the room, closed the door, and picked up the phone with the red blinking light on the desk.

"Hello, Langley. I need an hourly tracking report on agent Luke Stevens over the last twenty-four hours."

"Do you want me to send a copy of the report by email?" the communications officer asked.

"No. Just summarize what you read."

"Luke was in Beijing until four p.m. Tuesday your time. By six p.m., he was airborne over the Sea of Japan.

After that, we don't have any tracking until about seven a.m. this morning local time. At the last ping at eight a.m., his location moved roughly twenty miles northwest of his earlier location. Knowing he is at sea, he must have been picked up by a North Korean vessel. No one else would plot such a course."

"How long do you estimate before they make port?"

"At their current rate, they should make landfall late Wednesday night local time. They appear bound for a fishing village, Najin in North Korea."

"Thank you. This is helpful. Please update me with hourly details via intra-agency email," Tom said.

Tom left the quiet room and approached the duty officer.

"Do you know if any of our ships in the Sea of Japan reported intel on the commercial airliner that crashed last night?"

"We have a sub in the Sea of Japan that reported from sonar that the plane settled on the ocean bottom at roughly eight p.m. last night. Due to the typhoon overnight, nothing could be done about survivors."

"What about picking up survivors later today once the typhoon passes?"

"The sub has standing orders to run silent because of North Korean patrols. The waters west of the Yamato bank are shallow and the chances of an international incident are pretty high. Remember what happened to the USS Pueblo."

The Pueblo was a U.S. spy ship seized by North Korean patrol boats in international waters in January 1968 and one crew member was killed. The other eighty-two crew members were taken captive and tortured until December of that year, when they were released.

"Thanks. Call me on my cell number if any survivors are reported."

ACT TWO

Chapter Three

*B*y three p.m. on Wednesday afternoon, Captain Chǔ could see that the typhoon had passed. Whitecaps topped the waves even as the rain ceased, the wind slowed to a gentle breeze, and the sun illuminated the remaining clouds. A Chongjin class patrol boat appeared on the horizon. *Now the real trouble has come upon us.* The boat approached from the north and slowed as it drew near.

"Comrade Captain, identify yourself." The commander ordered in Korean using a hand-held megaphone. A crew member manned a machine-gun emplacement on the bow deck.

"I'm Captain Chǔ, boat registry 2850 out of Najin. I'm port-bound, carrying a registered load of squid."

"Registered? Are you sure that the squid is registered?"

"A government boat boarded us just west of the Yamato bank and we paid our loyalty tax. I have my receipt—do you want to see it?"

The commander's face tightened. "Don't patronize me or your boat will end up a ghost ship on a Japanese beach on the other side of the East Sea."

"You know, Comrade Commander, that the price of squid is down this month and our engine is unreliable, worthless. I'm not sure that my cargo will earn enough to buy gas for our next voyage," Captain Chǔ said.

The commander studied him, like a brigand assessing a passing caravan, "Go home, Captain Chǔ."

As the patrol boat sped away, Captain Chǔ's oldest son came on deck. "Father, are you sure you want to hide this foreigner? These patrol boat commanders are just looking for excuses to throw poor sailors into the sea, to seize and sell their cargos to the Russians, and to strip their engines for resale on the black market."

Captain Chǔ looked off into the distance, as in prayer, "Son, what would Jesus do?"

The ghost ship phenomena began when Western sanctions bankrupted the North Korean state fisheries fleet and North Korea began allowing private ownership of fishing boats. The old, poorly-maintained boats often broke down far at sea, the crews starved to death, and the boats washed up weeks later on Japanese beaches. While many North Korean products have been sanctioned over the years, Resolution 2371 of the United Nations Security Council that passed in August 2017 targeted seafood in response to North Korean missile tests.

§

Around four p.m. in Beijing, Tom called Harry on the dedicated cell phone he gave him.

"Harry, I have two concerns," Tom said without the small talk or formalities, as he might address a close friend.

"Luke's plane went down over the Sea of Japan. Although the media is blaming the typhoon, the plane was flying too high to have been affected significantly by weather. The pilot reported to the Tokyo control tower that they experienced catastrophic engine failure at forty thousand feet, which is cruising altitude for this model 747. We need to entertain the possibility that the plane was sabotaged with explosives triggered by a pressure fuse."

"You're probably right. What is your other concern?" Harry said.

"The only commercial boats in the Sea of Japan at the time of the crash were North Korean fishing boats. While we don't know that anyone survived, if they did, those fishermen are the ones most likely to know something."

"Let me see what I can learn from my contacts in North Korea. As long as we attribute the crash to bad weather or equipment failure, they should cooperate."

"Thanks."

§

Captain Chǔ docked his boat in Najin harbor at two a.m. Thursday morning. After tying off his rig, he instructed his sons, "Dress our guest in work clothes and a cap, and cover his face and hands with grease. If anyone asks, he is an injured crew member." Captain Chǔ turned to leave and hurried up the dock to the station office to make a call for help.

Arriving at the office, Captain Chǔ knocked on the door and said to the station master: "Excuse me, I have an injured crew member. May I borrow your telephone?"

"Certainly, step over into my office and shut the door."

Captain Chǔ called home and his wife answered. "How are you? Are the boys safe?"

"We're safe but we lost two crew members at sea and have another who is injured. Can you wake my father? I need his help with this injured crew member."

Chǔ waited patiently as several minutes passed. "Hello, son. I hear that you have an injured crew member. How can I help?" Comrade Chǔ inquired.

"Father, the injured man is a Westerner who survived a plane crash yesterday. He has yet to wake up and needs medical attention. How can we get him into the hospital without garnering attention?"

"Understood. I'll call my friends at the hospital and instruct them to send an ambulance to the dock and give the hospital guard some beer money. Many sailors have been injured in the typhoon, so this request won't arouse suspicion. I'll meet you at the hospital as soon as I can get dressed."

Captain Chǔ hung up the phone and asked the station master to direct the ambulance crew to his boat. Thanking him, he returned to the boat.

Several minutes passed before the ambulance arrived. Captain Chǔ assisted the ambulance crew in loading the plane-wreck survivor on a stretcher. When he was done, he turned to his sons, "Go home and get some rest. Let's get together to unload our cargo at nine a.m."

At that point, Captain Chǔ accompanied the survivor and the ambulance crew to the hospital, where he found his father waiting with the night-duty nurse. "How is our patient doing?" asked the nurse.

"He is still unconscious." Captain Chǔ said.

Comrade Chǔ leaned on the ambulance as he watched the ambulance crew put the survivor on a stretcher. As he waited, he began to reminisce with his son, "This ambulance brings back bitter memories. Most regional hospitals only have flatbed trucks to transport patients but our Supreme Leader designated Najin as a special economic zone back in the 1990s and gifted us with this imported, Russian ambulance. Nothing else came of that initiative and our hopes rusted like a cheap paint job."

Captain Chŭ nodded in agreement.

Comrade Chŭ sighed, "This ambulance carried our dreams driven by the engine of our hopes; it's an idol on wheels, whisking the unwary where they don't want to go."

"We have many such idols," Captain Chŭ continued. "Such dreams also weighed down the state fishing boat that now sits rusting at the dock. We vested our dreams in many programs, equipment, and heroes. It was comfortable sailing ships without having to worry about running out of fuel or being harassed by patrol boats looking to steal our cargoes. After drought, famine, and sanctions, our poverty is more conspicuous now that our idols have been unmasked, our hopes dashed, and our uniformed thieves have become more brazen."

"Najin is the city of the future and always will be," the nurse said, repurposing the Brazilian proverb as she shook her head.

In 1960, the gross domestic product per capita

(GDPC) of North and South Korea were roughly equal. More recent estimates (circa 2013) put the GDPC of South Korea at about eighteen times that of North Korea.

Like a Good Samaritan, Comrade Chŭ gave the nurse a generous bribe. "Our guest here survived a plane crash in the East Sea two nights ago. If he is to survive his stay in the hospital, he needs to be admitted without being registered or talked about. Place him in one of the quiet rooms in the back where he can be cleaned up without drawing attention to his appearance as a Westerner. If you spend more on this patient, let me know and I'll reimburse you when I return."

The nurse bowed and thanked Comrade Chŭ, "Everyone knows that you're a poor man with a big heart."

Comrade Chŭ stayed with the patient. The orderly wheeled him into a back room where the nurse cleaned him up, dressed him in some clean clothes, fed him some soup, and helped him to lie down and sleep. Captain Chŭ walked home, ate some cold, unsweetened corn porridge with dandelion tea, and went to bed.

Chapter Four

*A*t sunrise on Friday morning, Luke woke lying in a bed in a small room at the Provincial Hospital in Najin, North Korea, dressed in a white hospital gown. The room smelled of bleach. The only light came from two small windows in the ceiling, suggesting a room in the attic. The only furniture was a small wooden table that held a candle, pitcher of water, a washbowl, and a threadbare, white towel. A faded bedpan lay on the floor next to the bed. The gray walls were bare except for a color portrait of the two Kims, Kim Il-Sung and Kim Jong-Il, overlooking his bed.

A short, thin elderly Korean man sat in a chair next to his bed dressed in a baggy, long-sleeved black shirt and large, earthen-colored pressed pants held up by a tightly buckled, black-leather belt. One could only guess that one day, long ago, those clothes actually fit. Even the sandals he wore seemed designed for a larger person. As he stirred, an old man patiently watched him with large green eyes that looked out of keeping with his long gray hair and a Ho Chi Minh beard.

"Mr. Stevens, my name is Comrade Chǔ. Do you believe in miracles?" Chǔ said with a striking air of authority.

"Of course, Comrade Chǔ, I am a pastor." Luke paused, "Where am I? How do you know my name?"

"You're a guest at the Provincial Hospital in Najin in the Democratic People's Republic of Korea. I learned your name from the identity papers that you carried—they were all wet and I had to dry them out."

"North Korea? How did I get here?"

"Your plane crashed in the Korean East Sea. You spent a night floating in the sea and my son, Captain Chǔ, fished you out yesterday morning and brought you here. It is a miracle that you survived the plane crash and a miracle that you survived a night at sea in a typhoon. No one else is known to have survived. May I ask you a question?"

"Certainly. How can I help?"

"Who is Sarah? You spoke of her many times in your sleep."

"She was my ex-wife. I was flying her coffin back

to Washington for a funeral service and internment. After that, my fiancé, Abi, and I hope to be married over the Christmas holidays in McLean, Virginia."

"So it is true. You're the hero of Baltimore who saved the Premier's daughter, Abi—the whole world is looking for you."

"What? How do you know all this?" Luke said as if surprised that anyone missed him.

"Yesterday, the Chinese State Security Service sent a young man, Lei Han, here to interview hospital officials looking specifically for you."

Luke tried but failed in an attempt to sit up in bed. "What? The Director of Chinese State Security, Harry Bai, is looking for Lei Han, who is an accomplice in a failed *coup d'etat* in Beijing earlier this month. Lei Han is a fugitive from justice and known terrorist. Harry would never have sent him here looking for me."

"Relax, Mr. Stevens. No one knows you're here. You're an unregistered patient in a secluded room, off-limits to most hospital personnel. Lei Han has many powerful friends here in the drug trade and navy, but I'm not one of them."

"Wait a minute. Your name is Chǔ? I met a Pastor Chǔ in Northern Virginia. He helped me translate some inscriptions in a Chinese Bible that was given to my father in the Korean War."

Comrade Chǔ looked startled. He paused and said: "Inscriptions in a Chinese Bible? You must be the son of Phillip Stevens. I gave your father that Bible and wrote those inscriptions. He saved my life during the Korean War and, as a consequence, he was captured by the Chinese army near Jangjin Lake in 1950. This means that our meeting is another miracle."

Comrade Chǔ began to shed tears. "Pastor Chǔ must be my eldest son. My first wife was pregnant when she escaped south during the war. I always wondered whether she survived the war and had her baby. Now, he is a pastor like his father?" Chǔ whispered with his face in his hands.

"You are a pastor?"

"Officially, I'm a janitor in the hospital. Unofficially, I have baptized most of the babies in Najin. The government looks the other way because of those inscriptions in that Bible. I was a friend of the family of Mao Zedong. Our Supreme Leader even stops by informally to see me when he visits Najin or has a question about the Bible cited in Western media. Or maybe he just feels guilty about building the largest fentanyl lab in the world, right down the street, here in Najin. Who can say?"

"I would not have guessed there were any pastors in North Korea, because of its well-known persecution of Christians and official state atheism." Luke tried again to sit up, but fell back. Tired and desperate, he said, "What will become of me? How long will Abi wait before giving me up for dead?"

"Be patient. Turn to God in your pain and give it over to him. Meanwhile, we'll see what we can do," Comrade Chǔ assured him.

Still weak and delirious, Luke squirmed for few minutes before settling on his pillow and going back to sleep. Comrade Chǔ waited a few minutes to be confident that Luke was asleep before leaving to visit his son, Captain Chǔ.

§

In Beijing, the hospital discharged Harry, and he returned to work. Scrolling through the list of agents assigned to visit North Korea on his laptop in his office, he noticed that one of them left Pyongyang and made an unscheduled, unescorted trip to Najin, something unusual for Chinese agents in North Korea. After inquiring about the identity of this agent with his counterpart in Pyongyang, Mr. Park, he picked up the phone to call Tom.

"Hello, Tom? We have a problem. Lei Han has been sneaking around North Korea masquerading as an agent of Chinese State Security and searching for survivors of the plane crash."

"Do you think that this intel confirms that the plane was sabotaged?" Tom asked.

"Yes. Definitely. If Lei Han is involved, the motives could be both personal and political. If it is political, then Lei Han is more dangerous than we thought, because he has a mandate more extensive than just working for his old boss. It implies that Luke and Abi have become a symbol and target of opposition to the Premier's policy of detent between the United States and China. Are you in a hurry to return to Langley?"

"If I can be of service here, I'll hang around and invite Alex to assist."

"Thanks. You read my mind. We make a great team."

§

At the Beijing Hotel, Abi slept late with the covers pulled over her head. At ten o'clock, her mother, Rose, knocked on and opened her door.

"Abi, let's go out for tea," she said matter-of-factly as she walked into the room.

"Tea? Not tea. Anything but tea."

"What's going on here? You love tea." She sat on the bed and wrapped her arms around her daughter.

"It's all my fault." Abi began to cry, as her mother held and rocked her.

"What is your fault?"

"I went to Lei Han's teahouse and told him that Luke and I were engaged. He became angry and wanted to take revenge on Luke. Now Luke is dead and it is my fault."

"Did you tell Harry about this?"

"No. How could I? A whole plane full of people died. Luke is dead and Sarah will never get a funeral."

"Call Harry. He needs to know." Rose handed Abi a cell phone and folded her hands in her lap.

"You're right. Harry will know what to do."

Chapter Five

*A*round noon, Comrade Chǔ returned to find the nurse waking Luke. She gave Luke a sponge bath, dressed him in a fresh hospital robe, and sat him up in bed to eat a bowl of vegetable soup with a hint of rice and fish.

"How are you feeling?" Comrade Chǔ asked, eyeing the soup.

"I hate soup." The nurse fed him the last spoonful. "This is my penance for believing that I could make a difference in this world." The nurse took the spoon, the bowl, and a teacup, collected them on a tray, and carried them out of the room.

"Why are you feeling sorry for yourself? In Baltimore, you saved Abi's life and now she wants to marry you. What is the problem? Do you think that you're responsible for the plane crash?"

"Why did so many people have to die while I alone still live? Sarah's body is now lost at sea and I will never be able to bury her. How will I ever be able to find closure with our divorce, her untimely death, and now my grief?"

"Only God knows the answer to questions of life and death. Life is a gift. Be grateful for the time that you have been given," Comrade Chŭ said, projecting authority out of sync with his frail appearance.

"You are right, of course, but I still hate soup."

Comrade Chŭ pulled his chair closer to Luke's bed. "Let me change the subject. I spoke to my son, Captain Chŭ, who had some suggestions."

"Suggestions? What suggestions?"

"First, here is your cell phone. Improbably, it survived the plane crash because of the plastic wrapping. Type a message to Abi, but don't hit enter. Captain Chŭ will sail down close to the South Korea border tonight and once he gets close enough for a signal, he will send your message. Abi will be relieved to hear from you and, if someone nasty is monitoring your cell phone, they will think that you're in South Korea."

Luke typed: *I am safe. Sarah has been buried at sea. Tell Tom that Psalm 91 gives me consolation. See you soon, Love Luke.* Luke handed the phone back to Comrade Chŭ. "Was there another suggestion?"

"Yes. I would like you to meet my granddaughter, Chŭ Yong Dar. In English, she calls herself Ruth Chŭ. Her father, Captain Chŭ, wants her to smuggle you out of North Korea into China. In return, he asks that you help her to visit my son in Virginia and seek asylum in the United States."

"Smuggle?

"Yes. You can't stay here long. If the government finds you, you'll be our guest for years until the politics get sorted out. In China, you have friends who can help you return to a normal life. If Lei Han comes back and finds you, things could get messy."

"Ruth must be a tough cookie if you think she can smuggle me into China."

"Ruth is a force of nature, yet gentle and resourceful. In Pyongyang, the Central Broadcasting Committee of Korea recruited her to model for revolutionary posters that appear on state television and on every vacant wall in the country."

How is that possible? Luke thought. *A true North*

"If I call her today, she can take the train and be here on Sunday. She is currently a law student at Kim Il-sung University in Pyongyang, but earlier she worked for a pine mushroom collective near Chilbosan. In her role at the collective, she traveled all over Hamgyong Province looking for mushrooms and pine groves where they might be cultivated."

"Mushrooms?"

"Yes. Pine mushrooms. These mushrooms are valuable enough that local people smuggle them into China almost as often as illegal drugs, like fentanyl and cocaine. They can only be harvested in September and October so Ruth has a good excuse right now to leave school and visit us. Agricultural workers are routinely granted leave from their studies to bring in the harvest."

"Ruth sounds like someone I should meet. Let's be clear. I am not sure that she will be granted asylum, even with my help. Such decisions are above my pay grade."

"I understand. But it is obvious to me that your influence is greater than you think."

Chapter Six

*A*bout two a.m. Saturday morning, Captain Chǔ's boat arrived close to Kosong near the border with South Korea. Not used to the spectacle of city night lights, he imagined the city sparkling in the distance with lights reflecting off the water and clouds above. So mesmerized by the thought, he barely felt the waves slapping against the hull of his boat or noticed the putrid smell of fish that became more prominent as he approached a nearby fish processing plant. *Why must I smell fish while I remain cold and hungry?*

He turned on his running lights to avoid the drunken sport-boaters still on South Korean waters in spite of the late hour. It seemed incongruous to him, like a sick vision of heaven where just beyond the aurora of the holy city of God hangs a darkness broken only by the flashing of demonic fireflies. *Why am I condemned to live in the darkness?*

Captain Chǔ wondered what it must be like to enjoy electricity whenever you wanted, even at night. Or not need to worry about having fuel for the boat. Or time to enjoy something other than work. *Why are so many people in South Korea drunk and speeding around in expensive boats so carefree? Perhaps it is just capitalist propaganda hiding a darker truth, like the parades in Pyongyang staged only when the television cameras are turned on.*

Captain Chǔ cut his boat's engine, fished Luke's cell phone out of his pocket, and turned it on. It registered a weak signal with two bars. He pressed send on Luke's text, confirmed that it had been sent, and tossed the phone into the sea. It was not safe to have a cell phone, especially one that worked in South Korea. *Why can't I enjoy a phone with a compass, a GPS and photographs of happy people?*

Captain Chǔ caught himself daydreaming and felt in his bones the danger of being discovered by Northern patrol boats. He turned his boat around, cut off his running lights, and headed north to Najin. He was happy to be going home, but worried about what to say if he were stopped by a patrol boat and about how to pay for the fuel used for this evening's excursion. *Money, money, money. Who can afford all the bribes needed to get through a day at sea, let alone at night?*

§

Director Parks of the Reconnaissance General Bureau and a close confident of the Supreme Leader woke as usual when his telephone rang at five o'clock. This was not his usual call. His assistant informed him of the need to brief the Supreme Leader at six o'clock about new intel concerning the airline crash in the East Sea and reminded him that his limousine would pick him up at half-past five. He showered and dressed in his formal uniform. His wife set out a cup of coffee and a bowl of maize yuk (corn porridge) on the kitchen table, but he drank the coffee and left the *yuk* as he hurried out of his Pyongyang apartment to meet the limo. Exactly at half-past, Mr. Parks stepped into the limo door held open by his driver and he sat next to his assistant, who handed him a short briefing report. The driver took his seat and they departed for the ten-minute drive to the gym.

The gym stood on the campus of Kim Il-sung University and appeared inconspicuous, except for the presence of a dozen mean-looking, uniformed State Security

Department men from the Guard Command standing out front. When Mr. Parks' driver pulled up, two of these men ran over to inspect his passengers and opened the door for Mr. Parks, who saluted them and walked up to the gym. A second set of salutes and Mr. Parks entered the gym. Once inside, Mr. Parks took several steps forward towards a basketball court and stood at attention.

Precisely at six o'clock, the loudspeaker began playing, "Where Are You, Dear General," the theme music to a 1971 revolutionary opera credited to former Supreme Leader Kim Jong-Il. When it finished, the loudspeaker played "Do Prosper, Era of the Workers' Party" by the Moranbong Band, an all-girl group, like the Spice Girls. Supreme Leader Kim Jong-Un, North Korea's hereditary leader since 2011, organized this band the year after he assumed power.

In front of Mr. Parks stood the Supreme Leader dressed in gym clothes and holding a basketball under his left arm. Off to the side stood two attractive young, female servers in front of a long buffet table displaying perhaps twenty breakfast items, including maize *yuk*, *bulgogi* made from Kobe beef, sushi, Emmental cheese, dog meat soup, imported bauernbrot, *kimchi*, and some yogurts. Drinks included orange juice, several bottles of Cristal, snake wine, and various gourmet coffees from Brazil. The Supreme Leader motioned towards the buffet with his hand, handed the basketball to a server, picked up a serving plate, and invited Mr. Parks to join him for some breakfast.

"You must have something important to share, Mr. Parks, because you seldom join me for my morning exercise," the Supreme Leader said, cutting himself some cheese and bauernbrot.

"You requested an immediate briefing should there be any developments concerning the plane that crashed in the East Sea," Mr. Parks responded, as a server poured him coffee.

"Yes. What's happened?"

"Two items of interest have come up. First, the Premier's daughter received a text message earlier this morning from her fiancé, who had been on that flight. He appears to be alive somewhere in South Korea. If he survived the crash, perhaps others survived. Second, our telephone minders reported that your deceased nephew's fiancé received a request from her grandfather to make an unscheduled trip to Najin. Normally, such a request would not arouse any suspicion, but as you know she speaks flawless English and the request immediately followed the plane crash."

"So you believe these two events are related?"

"We don't know, but it is possible."

"Is it possible for me to meet with my nephew's fiancé before she departs? I never had a chance to offer her my condolences after my nephew was killed in the Baltimore incident last month."

"Her train departs for Najin this afternoon."

"Let's arrange to visit with her this afternoon at the train station."

§

Abi woke up as her cell phone beeped a notification. Though she was half asleep, when she read the text from Luke, she screamed and began jumping up and down. After a moment's thought, she ran out of her room and woke up her parents to read the text to them. When her father realized what the excitement was all about, he told her, "This text could be a fake."

"No, dad. Only Luke and Tom know about Sarah and the story behind Psalm 91."

"Story? What story?"

"Luke's father fought in the Korean War where he met a Korean pastor who gave him a Bible with an inscription that mentioned Psalm 91. Luke met the son of this pastor in northern Virginia, who translated the Mandarin and Korean inscriptions that were found in this Bible. In mentioning Psalm 91, Luke must imply that he met someone associated with that pastor in Korea."

"Interesting. Forward this text to Harry and explain the story behind it. Now excuse me, but I'm going back to bed."

Abi's mother followed her back to her room and waited while Abi forwarded the text and explained the story to Harry and Tom. She hugged Abi and they talked for half an hour before returning to bed. Unable to sleep, Abi tossed and turned all night, thinking, *Luke is alive, but is he okay?*

§

Saturday morning Tom read a transcript of Abi's text forwarded from CIA Headquarters in Langley and noticed the reference to Psalm 91. Curious to learn more, he called Langley to request Pastor Chŭ's cell phone number, which he dialed.

"Pastor Chŭ, this is Tom Smith with the State Department's missing persons office. Do you remember talking with Pastor Stevens about inscriptions in a Chinese Bible?"

"How could I forget? The inscriptions in that Bible gave me hope that my father, the other Pastor Chŭ, survived the Korean War and remains alive."

What can you tell me about Psalm 91?"

"Psalm 91 is a favorite psalm among Pentecostals like my father because of the protection and comfort God offers during stressful times. Verse seven is particularly popular: *A thousand may fall at your side, ten thousand at your right hand, but it will not come near you.* According to the inscriptions, this verse motivated the Chinese

Captain to seek out my father during the war."

"Pastor, does the city of Najin, North Korea, mean anything to you?"

"Yes. Before the Korean War, my father pastored a church in Najin."

"What else can you tell me about your father?"

"The name, Chǔ, isn't Korean, it's Chinese so if you find a Chǔ in Korea, we're probably related because the name is rare and Koreans don't mix well with Chinese socially. In part because of our Chinese heritage, my father is a polyglot, speaking Korean, English, and Chinese."

"Pastor Chǔ, no promises, but we believe that members of your family still live in Najin."

"Oh, my goodness. Do you know any more details about them?"

"No. Not at this point. If I learn more information, I'll get back to you."

"Thank you. Thank you." Pastor Chǔ repeated.

§

When he woke up on Saturday morning, Harry

found Abi's two texts on his cell phone. Abi's disclosure that she had visited with Lei Han combined with the report of Lei Han's travel to North Korea convinced Harry that Luke's plane had been sabotaged. Abi's receipt of Luke's text message led him to inquire about its South Korean origin. He called Tom.

"Good morning, did you hear about the text from Luke?" Harry said.

"Yes. Thanks for the call; I was about to call you," Tom said.

"A cell tower near Kosong in South Korea picked up the message around two o'clock this morning."

"If Luke were in South Korea, why wouldn't he just call and make reservations to return to Beijing?" Tom said.

"Perhaps, he is injured and is texting from a hospital."

"I suspect that if he were truly safe, he would have sent a more detailed account. Why, for example, did he only send one text? Did Abi text him back?"

"She tried, but Luke's cell phone has apparently

been turned off. Also, yesterday Abi admitted to me that she spoke to Lei Han earlier this week. I also heard that Lei Han was snooping around North Korea this week after the plane crash," Harry said.

"Wow. Now, things are starting to make sense. Luke is a clever guy. He must be hiding somewhere in North Korea and he may even know that Lei Han is after him. If so, the text may be a head fake to throw people off his trail."

Harry scratched his head. "Head fake?"

"A head fake is a basketball move where you pretend to go one way with your head but actually move your body in the opposite direction. If the text suggests he is in South Korea, then my guess is Luke is headed north into China. How would the North Koreans react if they found Luke alive?"

"I don't know, but I'll inquire."

"One more thing that you should not share with the North Koreans. Luke's text mentions Psalm 91, which is a reference to an old war story. Luke's father met a Pastor Chǔ during the Korean War, who may still be alive and living near Najin, North Korea. It is possible that he is caring for Luke and helping him to get out of North Korea," Tom said.

"Interesting. Perhaps we can help Luke execute this head fake because we may not be the only ones who have heard about this text. What if we suggest to the media that we're looking in South Korea for leads on Luke's whereabouts?"

"Good idea. Just make it look like the disclosure was leaked."

Harry laughed. "Ha, ha. A good tea must seep, as the saying goes. Beijing is the leak capital of the world."

ACT THREE

Chapter Seven

Saturday afternoon Harry called Abi, "I'm scheduling a press briefing at three o'clock this afternoon here in my Beijing office on the plane crash, the hunt for the wreckage, and the search for possible survivors. All the major media outlets will be present. Because Luke was on that plane, your presence would be helpful in raising the visibility of our efforts."

"What about the text? Have you located Luke?" Abi said.

"I'll leave this afternoon for Seoul, South Korea, to take part in the search. Perhaps he washed up on a beach and has been taken to a local hospital. It is unclear why his whereabouts haven't been officially reported," Harry said.

"Okay, I'll attend the briefing, but I want to go with you to Seoul."

"Sure. I would enjoy your company on this trip and the South Koreans will be more willing to cooperate knowing your active interest and participation in the search. As for the briefing, I'll send a car to pick you up."

"Thanks. See you soon."

§

Lei Han, who wore a white shirt and tie with an official-looking, two-piece suit, traveled by train from Najin to Pyongyang late Saturday afternoon where two uniformed officers of the Reconnaissance General Bureau met him at the station and escorted him to their offices for a debriefing. They walked him through security without stopping and took the elevator to the top-floor conference room. In the room, photographs of the two Kims overlooked a long table with tenth-century *Hwarang* helmets and swords hanging on either side. An image of this display is used on official agency documents. There Lei Han shook hands with Director Parks, who wore an almost-identical two-piece suit.

"Mr. Han, please have a seat," Mr. Parks said, directing him to a chair around a large conference table. "How is your cat, Mr. Premier?"

Lei Han grinned. "Because of his name, he thinks he is in charge!"

"Because time is short, please tell me: What have

you learned during your travels? Did you find any survivors of the plane crash?" Mr. Parks inquired.

"Thank you for your interest," Lei Han began. "As you know, the crash occurred over the East Sea close to the Yamato bank. The prevailing currents would take any survivors or debris north from the crash and east towards Japan. However, there was some chance that a survivor may have been picked up by North Korean fishermen. Consequently, I concentrated on visiting hospital officials and fishermen along with the East Sea coastal villages, towns, and cities, but no survivors were reported."

"Apparently, one person, a Mr. Luke Stevens, survived. Our electronic surveillance picked up a text message in English early Saturday morning from Mr. Stevens in South Korea. Because of the two a.m. timing, he must have just arrived." Mr. Parks passed a written transcript of the message across the table to Lei Han.

"Has his presence in South Korea been confirmed?"

"In a public briefing this morning in Beijing, your boss Bai Cheng (a.k.a. Harry Bai) stated that he plans to travel to South Korea this evening to investigate."

"I'll check with my office. Perhaps, they could use some assistance," Lei Han said.

Mr. Parks smiled and stood to shake hands with his guest. Officers escorted Lei Han back to the airport.

§

Mr. Parks returned from the conference room to his office and called the limousine pool. Minutes later, his telephone rang and he took the elevator down to the basement parking lot and stepped into a waiting limousine that drove him to the train station.

From his limousine, Mr. Parks observed Chǔ Yong Dae enter the train station. She wore a white blouse, red scarf, and black pencil skirt, like many other students, but she stood taller and healthier than other women with her hair shining against a dull sea of split ends— the consequence of a prolonged, protein-deficient diet. She walked through crowds like a green Statue of Liberty cutting through a gray fog. Men turned their heads to look; women gasped, recognizing the woman pictured in so many official posters and billboards.

Next to the ticket counter, Mr. Parks directed two uniformed officers of the Reconnaissance General Bureau to approach Ms. Chŭ and escort her to a room, opening the door for her and remaining outside. Mr. Parks followed her into the room where, after bowing, she took a seat at a table opposite the Supreme Leader.

"Please excuse this little detour from your trip home this evening. We'll not keep you long and we have instructed the train engineer to delay departure until you board, Mr. Parks said.

The Supreme Leader sighed. "You perhaps heard about the plane crash into the East Sea this week. We aren't involved in any way, but the site of this crash is most embarrassing for our country. We believe that the plane was sabotaged by a dissident Chinese group linked with the Triads, who recently attacked the government and even now are attempting to assassinate the future son-in-law of the Premier, a Mr. Luke Stevens. We believe that he survived the crash and is in hiding in North Korea, having been rescued by one of our fishermen, perhaps even your own father."

Chŭ Yong Dae nodded. A poker face masked her emotions.

The Supreme Leader looked surprised by her composure, perhaps expecting an emotional response to his last comment. He paused and said, "Our country's only serious ally and trading partner is the People's Republic of China, who saved our military from certain defeat by U.S. forces during the Fatherland Liberation War, which the Americans call the Korean War. The sabotage of a commercial airliner near our air space appeared designed to embarrass our country and shift blame away from those responsible. Assisting the Chinese Premier's future son-law to return safely to China will curry favor with the Premier, regardless of any public statements."

The Supreme Leader glanced at Mr. Parks and said, "Because of the politically sensitive nature of the matter, we can't officially offer Mr. Stevens sanctuary or assistance. Unofficially, if you hear about him during your visit home, please let us know. Just so you know, members of the smuggling directive security service, who normally police trafficking, will be in training the next two weeks and border guards twenty kilometers north and south of Chongsong will be restricted to base evenings during this period, ostensibly to prepare for celebrating this year's Party Foundations Day."

"Thank you for sharing these things with me," Ms. Chŭ said.

The Supreme Leader stood and his face turned sad, "My condolences on the recent death of your fiancé." After that, he shook Ms. Chŭ's hand and left the room.

Mr. Parks escorted Ms. Chŭ back to the train platform, bowed, and said his goodbyes. He remained on the platform to make sure that she safely boarded, then he notified the engineer of her boarding and returned to the limousine, where the Supreme Leader waited. He took a seat next to him.

§

On his voyage back to Najin, Captain Chŭ's boat experienced engine trouble and was delayed all morning. By late Saturday afternoon, he was still fifty kilometers from port. A Chongjin class patrol boat approached from the east, slowing as it approached. As it came alongside his boat, he realized that it was the same patrol boat that had stopped him on Wednesday.

"Comrade captain, we meet again," the commander said, speaking into his megaphone. "Where's your crew?"

"I experienced engine trouble and sent my men home in another boat," Captain Chǔ said.

"Then, you'll not mind if I inspect your catch."

"Not at all. You're welcome to come aboard, but we caught nothing."

The Commander chuckled, pretending to be amused, "Ah-ha. So I caught you trafficking people to South Korea?"

"Smuggling people? You have known me since we worked together in the state fishing industry together and, now, you accuse a former boatswain's mate being a traitor and a capitalist?"

"Obviously. How else could you earn enough money to operate such a fancy boat and hire your own crew after capitalist sanctions bankrupted the state fishing industry in 2017? You know the penalty for trafficking. Hand over your earnings or I'll seize your boat."

"I have no earnings because I'm not a trafficker."

"Shoot him," the commander ordered the deck gunner, who fired a burst from his machine gun.

Captain Chŭ fell mortally wounded into the sea and disappeared from view.

The commander's men boarded and searched the boat. One man found a Bible, looked both ways, and quietly hid it under his shirt. They found nothing else of value and stripped the engine for sale on the black market. They lashed the two boats together and spent forty-five minutes hoisting the engine on to the patrol boat over rolling decks. Afterwards, they set Captain Chŭ's boat adrift and sped away.

That evening the commander cabled his superiors about the incident, saying, *Captain Chŭ, boat registry 2850 out of Najin, was caught trafficking people into South Korea and was shot attempting to escape.*

Lei Han's friends in the North Korean navy texted him the report. He took it as confirmation that Luke had been smuggled by boat into South Korea.

Chapter Eight

Saturday evening, Tom met with Alex over dinner, sitting at a small table in her hotel room in Beijing. "I want you to head up a joint Chinese-American medical team to travel to the city of Yanji in Jilin providence in northern China. The cover story is that you're researching rare cases of infant hepatitis in rural areas, but the real purpose is to prepare to receive Luke, should he succeed in smuggling himself out of North Korea." Tom took a bite of his salad and chewed a bit.

"Local officials in China are notoriously independent and have been known to shakedown visiting researchers," Alex said.

"You'll have a side-arm and a small security detail to avoid mishaps with local authorities. You'll be carrying a highly classified tracking device disguised as medical equipment. Only you'll know it's true purpose. No one can know that we're able to track our agents, so the device includes a self-destruct mechanism. It can be activated remotely with a special pen or triggered automatically in the event of tampering." Tom said.

"You do realize that I have never worked as an operative," Alex said, giving Tom a sideways glance.

"Aren't you the one who double-tapped a terrorist last week and foiled a bombing the week before?"

"That was different. The terrorist spoiled my dinner and the bomber tried to ruin my day," Alex added, trying to mask her enthusiasm for having had an active role in helping rescue Luke.

"¡Dios mio! You're a natural field agent and one of the most focused individuals I have ever worked with. The key point for this mission is that Luke knows and trusts you. Coming out of North Korea, he may be reluctant to follow directions from a stranger, especially one who doesn't speak English well. He may also have injuries that need attention."

"Okay, okay."

"Just so you know, when we get stateside, I'm putting you in for an award and promotion. We need more people like you."

Alex smiled. "Thanks Tom. It's fun working with someone who knows what they are doing and how to motivate people. But you have to know that I have been worried sick about Luke and will do what it takes to return him home safely."

"Hmm. You seem to have more than a passing interest in Luke. Am I wrong?" Tom said.

"It's not what you think. Luke's son and I were classmates at the Naval Academy and we had a son together. That makes Luke the grandfather of my son, Philip. Luke is family, even though he only learned the truth of our connection in recent weeks. We're still working through the implications of our relationship."

"Thanks. I didn't know. I didn't mean to pry into personal matters."

"Not to worry. I should have told you a long time ago."

§

When Chǔ Yong Dae arrived at eleven p.m. Saturday, she found her grandfather, Comrade Chǔ, waiting for her at the Najin train station. She wondered why the ninety-year-old man came alone to meet her so late at night, but out of respect said nothing.

As they walked home in the evening fog, he explained, "Yong Dae, thank you for traveling promptly from Pyongyang to see me. I have someone that I want you to meet. He is an American and a survivor of the plane crash earlier this week that your father rescued at sea. I want you to escort him over the border into China."

"Where's my father? Why has he not come to meet me?"

"Your father is several hours overdue from his last voyage."

"This isn't good. If the patrol boats detained him, following protocol, the police will set up roadblocks and raid the house at five a.m. We must hurry. As a precaution, the entire family must visit my mother's sister tonight and I must take this American and go. What is his name?"

"Luke Stevens."

"The Chinese Premier's prospective son-in-law?" Yong Dae cringed, remembering her meeting at the train station and realizing the enormity of the request that was being made. The Supreme Leader must have known all along.

"Yes. The whole world is looking for him."

"Take me straight to the hospital. Is he healthy enough to travel?"

"Yes. He remains weak but has recovered from the plane crash and his time at sea."

"We'll need to borrow a driver and an ambulance tonight for a trip to the clinic in Undok. Tell the driver that Luke and I are nurses who have been assigned to work there for the next three months. We'll dress in nurses' uniforms and carry along a change of clothes, preferably worker's uniforms, so we'll need backpacks. The driver will return before any morning police raids. Nothing will seem suspicious because ambulances perform such duties all hours of the day and night."

"What about your father?"

"If my father comes home safely, he will understand. If not, at least we'll not be caught unaware."

"I have always told people how perceptive and resourceful you are."

Yong Dae and her grandfather arrived at the family's apartment, grabbed a few things, and ate some dinner. When they were alone, her grandfather gave Yong Dae a small pistol and a wad of twenty-dollar bills. He told her: "You may need these—Life on the road can be stressful and dangerous. Travel to America to visit your uncle, if you're able."

After eating, she gave her mom some money and helped her pack a few things for the trip over to her aunt's apartment. She then walked over to the hospital with her grandfather. Once inside the building, she disappeared for a few minutes to visit the hospital laundry and returned wearing gray scrubs with a tapered, white lab coat. She walked over to meet Luke.

"Luke, this is my granddaughter, Yong Dae. In English, she goes by Ruth. She is going to guide you on your trip to China."

"Ruth, thanks for your help. You don't look like a typical nurse."

"Neither do you. Here, put this on." Ruth handed Luke scrubs and a lab coat to match her own. "We need to leave promptly to avoid any mishap."

Luke walked behind a nearby partition, slipped into the nurse's uniform, and came out with his hospital gown in hand. "What do I do with my gown?"

"Give it to me." Ruth took the gown, walked behind the nurse's station, and threw it into a hamper. Returning, she said, "When we're around people, stand up, bend over a bit, and hold this backpack up in front of your face and let me do the talking."

"That is easy. I do not understand a word of Korean."

Ruth turned to her grandfather. "Where can I find a typewriter and some paper?"

He guided her to an empty nurse's station, where she typed out a transit request and approval to travel to Undok. "Let's go find that driver. After we leave, you go stay with the family for the weekend."

Grandfather directed Ruth and Luke to the emergency department, where he said goodbye, hugged Ruth, and shook Luke's hand before departing.

Ruth approached the duty nurse and handed her the forged transit orders. The nurse called a driver and they left by ambulance around one a.m. for the ninety-minute ride to Undok. Ruth and Luke climbed in the back of the ambulance as if they had traveled this way many times before. They made themselves comfortable, pretending to be relaxed, and quickly nodded off.

§

At four a.m. Sunday at the hotel in Beijing, Tom called Alex and woke her. "Alex, sorry to wake you. Langley notified me that Luke has been tracked approaching Chongsong, North Korea, a staging area for smuggling people and contraband into China. I need your team to fly to Yanji ASAP."

"No problem. I'm on it. Talk to you as soon as I get details together."

"Thanks." Tom hung up and called Harry at his hotel in Seoul.

"Harry, I apologize for the early call. I have asked Alex to form a medical team to fly to Yanji as soon as arrangements can be made. The stated purpose is to investigate an outbreak of infant hepatitis in the Jilin province, but the real purpose is to receive Luke if he crosses the

Tumen River into China near Chongsong, North Korea. Do you have people who might serve with this medical team? They will also need a security detail to keep them company."

"I'll fly there today to organize the security detail. You should come; I could use your insights. Because this is ostensively a medical mission, Abi will, I'm certain, insist on coming," Harry said. "Otherwise, we have a bilingual doctor who can assist."

"Okay. I'll tag along with Alex. Before you go, thank you for assisting with the head fake. It bought us some time that may prove critical."

"No problem. See you in Yanji." Harry hung up.

Chapter Nine

Ruth woke Sunday morning with the sun in her eyes. Looking out the ambulance window, she recognized the mountain pass overlooking a distant Chongsong. She grabbed her backpack, reached inside, and shoved her pistol into the pocket of her nurse's jacket. Then, she woke Luke, motioned to him to be quiet, and peered around the corner at the driver.

"This isn't the clinic in Undok. Where have you taken us?" Ruth asked the driver.

"Undok doesn't need nurses right now so we have been diverted to the hospital in Chongsong. It's a much better assignment," the driver said.

Ruth reached over the seat and placed her pistol next to his head. "Nurses aren't given work assignments by ambulance drivers. Now you're going to tell the real reason we're headed to Chongsong."

"No. No. That is the truth."

Ruth chambered a round in her pistol and gave the driver a shove with the end of its barrel. "One more lie and I'll shoot your head off."

§

From the back of the ambulance, Luke recognized Ruth's pistol as the same 25-caliber, Fabrique Nationale Baby Browning model pistol that killed his son earlier that year in Baltimore. *Who is this woman? Where is she taking me?*

He said nothing, but his heart started to race. For the first time since waking up in the hospital, he was afraid. *Is it my destiny to be shot by the same weapon that killed my son?*

§

Ruth gave the ambulance driver another shove with her pistol.

"Okay. Okay. The military police are offering a generous reward for Americans who survived the plane crash in the East Sea this week. Human traffickers pay almost as much for young nurses, who are sold as wives to rich Chinese."

"So the female nurse's shortage in North Hamgyŏng province has finally been explained. Who does this?" Ruth said, knowing that desperate people will do anything to earn a few U.S. dollars to feed their starving families.

"The hospital in Chongsong pays a bounty to drivers that divert nurses to them," the driver explained.

"How does the hospital get away with open trafficking?" Ruth asked.

"They pay their loyalty tax and introduce local police to the young women, who are eager to get out of North Korea. Everyone gets something." The driver smiled. "If the parents of these nurses ask questions, they are told that their daughter escaped to China, which is almost true. If they persist in asking questions, they are threatened with arrest. Most parents don't question the lies."

"Why are military police in Chongsong?"

"The military police have recently been stationed in Chongsong to keep an eye on the border guards, who have been known to take bribes from local smugglers. They even place snipers on local ridges to shoot people who try to cross the Tumen River during the day."

Ruth ordered the driver to pull over and get out of

the ambulance. Before he could say a thing, she jumped out of the ambulance, grabs his keys, shoves twenty dollars into his hand, and pointed to a nearby cooperative farm. "Walk over to that farm and tell them that your ambulance broke down. Ask them to fix you lunch, then walk to the hospital in Chongsong, where you'll find your ambulance. Take your time. All this should take you until late afternoon if you know what is good for you."

Ruth watched as the driver walked off towards the farm. He neither hurried nor seemed particularly worried, as if he had pistols pointed at his head every day. Once he was out of sight, she moved up and sat in the driver's seat.

Luke moved up and sat in the front seat next to Ruth, who prepared to start the ambulance. "Why did you give the driver lunch money?" He asked, wondering when he too would get lunch but understanding implicitly that lunch was not in the program. Perhaps neither was dinner.

Ruth gave Luke a puzzled look. "I didn't need to shoot him. With money in his hand, he will think that today is his lucky day that he has money for lunch and will forget that I put a gun to his head and borrowed his ambulance. Don't worry that he will report us—he knows that the police will likely steal everything he has before even pretending to listen to his story. He is better off keeping his mouth shut and keeping the money."

"Are you ready?" Ruth started the engine and drove the ambulance further towards Chongsong.

§

At six a.m. Sunday morning in Seoul, Harry telephoned Abi in her hotel room. "I apologize for the early call, but time is short. I'm flying to Yanji, China at ten a.m. to organize a security detail to accompany a medical team headed by your friend, Alex. The team will officially be researching infant hepatitis in the rural Jilin province. Unofficially, they will be positioning to intercept Luke, should he get smuggled across the Tumen River near Chongson, North Korea. The medical team needs a Chinese doctor to support this work. Are you interested?" Harry asked.

"Absolutely. I can be packed and ready to leave

in fifteen minutes." Abi said.

"Good. Let's meet outside in front of the *Haechi* statue."

"What is an *Haechi*?"

"An *Haechi* is a mythical beast out of Manchuria. It has the body of a lion, an ox tail, and a coat of metal armor. It is intelligent, understands human speech, and acts like a guard dog in the cause of justice. It is believed to eat fire, which is why these statues often appear in front of buildings."

"So statues are cheaper than fire insurance?" Abi grinned.

§

In the next room, a twenty-something female associate of Lei Han who had bugged Abi's room and telephone picked up the phone and called him. "Mr. Han, sorry for the early call. The Minister of State Security and the Premier's daughter are taking a ten a.m. flight to Yan-ji, China, to look for Mr. Stevens."

"Make flight arrangements for two to Yanji, China, preferably on the same flight. You'll pose as my dutiful daughter who is taking her unfashionable, gray-haired father to visit country relatives," Lei Han said.

"Unfashionable, gray-haired father?"

"Yes. The Minister of State Security and the Premier's daughter both know me, so I need to disguise myself. Wear a bow in your hair and pick up a tight-fitting tie shirt from Seoul National University to wear on the flight to draw attention away from me and give the appearance that you're a South Korean student."

"Right!"

§

As Ruth drove along the ridge-line of mountains overlooking a distant Chongsong, illumined by the morning sun, Luke looked out to see desert rock, dust, and sand broken only by an occasional oasis of succulents and hardy trees wherever a smudge of water could be found. In the morning mist, these patches of green might be mistaken for a more hospitable area. Soon the barren landscape gave way to an expansive pine forest.

"We can't cross the Tumen River until dark this evening. This implies that we have the whole day ahead of us to find our way to the river. Would you like to visit a park?" Ruth smiled.

"Sounds like fun, but is it safe to take the ambulance into a park? Won't we look out of place?"

"Normally, it's deserted, except for a few mushroom hunters, because few villagers have energy left over after work to climb the ridge and walk a couple of miles without good cause. If anyone asks, we can tell them that we stopped for a break because we aren't expected in Chongsong until late afternoon." Ruth turned on a dirt road and headed into the woods, kicking up dust the whole way.

A mile or so down the road, they came to a clearing with an old stone building on the far side. Given the water fountain out front and the adjacent cemetery, it was obviously a church that dated back before the communist takeover. A young man standing at the front door disappeared inside when he saw them coming, like a lookout hurrying to make a report.

"Perhaps, we can learn a few things from that fellow. If we're lucky, he can direct us to someone who might offer us breakfast." Ruth pulled over in front of the building. "Stay with the ambulance while I go in and check out this guy." Ruth checked her pistol, got out of the ambulance, and walked into the building.

§

Luke was confused. On the one hand, Ruth seemed transparently gracious and on his side. On the other hand, the pistol hinted at another truth dark and insidious, like the revolution posters that he had seen on the streets in Najin. *How could both be the same Ruth?*

Luke waited a minute before stepping out of the ambulance, Thirsty, he walked over, cupped his hand, and scooped up the cool mountain water bubbling up in the center of the fountain. As he drank the water, he noticed a copper coin in the fountain, which he fished out—it was an American penny dated 1929. Looking around the fountain, he noticed that weeds and a few wildflowers grew thicker close to the fountain where the wind occasionally sprinkled a few drops of water. *How could this tiny garden persist so many years without a caretaker?*

§

Ruth opened the church door to find a room about eighty feet long and twenty feet wide. It had oak flooring, stained-glass windows on both sides with wooden benches against each of the walls under the windows. The bench on the left held three young, female nurses dressed just like Ruth in white uniforms and carrying a few personal things in small backpacks like schoolchildren. The young man paced back and forth across the room before walking over to Ruth.

"Where's your driver?" The young man asked.

I must have stumbled into a scheduled detour on the road to Chongsong, Ruth thought. "My brother got sick and asked me to fill in."

The young man motioned for Ruth to follow him out the back door of the church. Outside he said: "Your brother is a coward. The Party Foundation Day preparations announced for this week and next are a ruse to trap smugglers. He is pretending to be sick so that you'll be the one going to prison." The young man went on. "Your parents must have wanted another girl because he obviously flunked out of nursery school and played with baby-dolls."

This prejudiced young man is clueless, but perhaps he can be helpful, pondered Ruth. "I have no idea. He said that you would explain everything I need to know."

The young man continued. "He would. I hope he chokes on tainted water and sawdust stuffing." The young man persisted in pacing back and forth.

"So what must I do?" Ruth asked.

"The nurses are expected to attend a dinner at the Chongsong Hospital at six p.m. and get their photographs taken to send to their parents. From seven to ten p.m., they are invited to a zipper party with local guards and police. At ten, you'll drive them to the Tumen River. Follow the river road north one kilometer past the fence and let them cross. Chinese police will pick them up at eleven on the other side."

"Zipper party? So our own police and soldiers shamelessly prefer their grandparents' Japanese surnames and have turned Korean girls into comfort women?"

"You know, we have to support our men in uniform." The young man smiled slyly. "Shame is for traditionalists. Thanks to the one-child policy in China and Western sanctions, we both know that a homely Geisha in China eats better than a flashy nurse in North Korea."

Ruth turned to look out a window, hiding her anger and disgust. *I'm supposed to be a corrupt communist—I can't afford real opinions and emotions.* Slipping back into her smuggler persona, she raised her voice to ask, "So why drive a kilometer past the fence?"

"The fence runs one kilometer north of Chongsong. The shoreline for the first kilometer past the fence is lined with pits to trap people who try to cross the river in the dark on their own. Every morning, the border guards fish those who tried to flee out of the pits. The women are trafficked into China and the men are sent to prison camps."

Walk like a smuggler; talk like a smuggler, Ruth mused. "Let's get down to business. How much do I get paid for transporting these women?"

The young man reached in his pocket, pulled out a wad of dollars, and handed it to Ruth.

"Do you have lunch for the nurses?"

The young man handed her his backpack.

"Why do you meet in this park?" Ruth asked.

"It's quiet and deserted. No one comes here, not even the police. Well, almost no one. If you see anyone at this time of year, you can bet that they smuggle mushrooms."

"Good. You can take off. We'll hang out here to enjoy the peace until around five. We'll set off in time to arrive at the hospital around 5:30 p.m. This will give the nurses time to clean up before dinner."

"Check out the apple and apricot trees out back along the stream next to the path. The water is drinkable and further downstream it is surrounded by wild blueberries and blackberries this time of the year." The young man left the church and walked off down the same path toward Chongsong.

Ruth walked back into the church and approached the nurses.

"Good morning. My name is Ms. Kim. How are you doing?"

"What are we doing here? We were supposed to

be transported to Chongsong Hospital to start work."

"This is a lunch break while we wait for others to join us." Ruth handed them the backpack with food. The nurses fought over the backpack like wolves sparring over a deer carcass. After a point, they divided up the food and sat alone in silence to eat their shares.

"Does anyone here know how to drive?" Ruth asked.

One nurse nodded and Ruth handed her keys to the ambulance. "Wait here until 5:30 p.m. in case others show up. Then drive to Chongsong Hospital where they will hold a dinner in your honor at 6 p.m."

Ruth walked to the door and hesitated. *I have to be honest with these poor girls.* She turned to the nurses. "What would you say if I told you that Chongsong Hospital is a front for human traffickers who will sell you as brides in China?"

"You're a shameless liar. No way. That is such a rude joke. Why would you say such a thing?" The nurses said one after the other.

"Enjoy your lunch." Ruth turned, pushed the door

open, and left the church to rejoin Luke.

§

Ruth and Luke walked down the path that the young man had taken, picking and eating apples, apricots, and berries along the way. When they came to the edge of the forest, they stopped to change into the workers' clothes they had brought with them. Ruth placed the nurse's uniforms and her pistol in their backpacks and hid them in the underbrush.

Sitting down next to a pine tree, Ruth said, "According to the young man, the guards and local police will be at the hospital at seven. That means that we have a risk-free opportunity to walk around Chongsong to the Tumen River and wait on the hillside for them to transport the nurses to the river at ten. With luck, we can watch the smugglers cross the Tumen River and the Chinese police pick them up, avoiding both. Let's pray that we'll not be reported before then. We don't want the police to drop everything to search for us. That would negate our intel, mess up our timetables, and leave us without a viable strategy to avoid capture."

"Great plan." After a few minutes, Luke added, "Has anyone told you that you are a distracting woman?" Luke said, as he sat next to Ruth and leaned with her against a tree.

Ruth's jaw dropped. "Focus on the mission, young man." Ruth paused, then responded coyly, "In case you're wondering, I was engaged to be married until my fiancé was killed in Baltimore earlier this month."

Luke snapped his head around to look at her. "I am so sorry." Luke took her hand and looked in her eyes. "Now I am embarrassed. Why are you helping me?"

"It was an arranged marriage. I hardly knew my fiancé. He was a black sheep in a powerful family used to getting their way. My family could not easily refuse their proposal. As it turned out, he died in the line of duty. His father is proud; his mother gets a small pension; and I get to play the almost-grief-stricken, free woman. Because you asked, I'm helping you because my grandfather asked me to." Ruth blushed and averted her eyes as she shifted to lean closer to him.

"Oh, okay," Luke said, a bit slow on the uptake.

He suddenly realized that Ruth was the real deal. The pistol revealed a strong side of her and her family loyalties another. Much like Chinese Confucianism spawned complex, multifaceted, deep personalities, the stresses in North Korean culture spawned bipolar personas alien to straightforward, often superficial Americans, not accustomed to subtlety and secret-keeping. Luke found himself drawn in, as with the gardens in Beijing.

"How did you meet your fiancé, Abi?"

"It's complicated. We met online. It was on our first date when I prevented Abi's abduction in the coffeehouse shootout. All I remember is that I woke up in the hospital shot in the back, traumatized without any memory of most of what happened. Two weeks ago, at my dad's funeral, she invited me to Beijing, and then this week she proposed marriage and I accepted. If our whirlwind romance seems abrupt, you might say that we have lived our lives recently in dog years." Luke could only bring himself to tell Ruth the official story, not the whole story, of his relationship with Abi.

"I am hearing drama; I don't sense any real romance. It's like you and I both have been committed to arranged marriages. Me because I'm a woman in North Korea; you because you don't know who you are. Perhaps, our meeting isn't an accident," Ruth said.

Arranged marriage? Me? Luke's mind began to wander. *Should I tell her who I am and who Sarah is? Did our failed marriage leave me vulnerable, emotionally wounded?* Time passed while Luke shifted around nervously. "Abi is a great gal and I love her. I am sure that my disappearance is driving her crazy." Luke sensed that Ruth saw through his superficial statement but she was not about to let go of their evolving connection.

"Relax. Don't worry so much. Let's hang out here until it gets dark, which is at about a quarter to six. In the meantime, close your eyes a minute," Ruth rubbed dirt on Luke's face and hands like a mother preparing her child for school. "If we meet anyone, don't talk and bend over a bit, so you don't look so tall. You should look like a shy farm worker, hard as it might seem to believe," she said with a wry smile.

A few minutes after Ruth covered his face with

dirt, Luke found the tension in his body melting away. He was too tired not to relax. In a state of semi-consciousness, he watched a distant train enter the Chongsong station, stop, let people off, and take on new passengers. Local people hurried this way and that throughout the town returning home after work. Further off against the sunset, the Tumen River flowed northeast from the mysterious Paektu Mountain in the south towards Russia in the north, passing Chongsong with shallow rapids winding down the valley flanked by sandy beaches and fencing to prevent easy crossing.

Ruth quietly sang a children's verse:

"Tumen, Tumen take me away

From Paektu Mountain to Russian bay

Don't leave Chosen children

to starve in a land not free."

Ruth took Luke's hand and leaned against him, expressing intimacy uncommon in Korean culture. Exhausted, Luke shut his eyes.

ACT FOUR

Chapter Ten

*A*t noon on Sunday, Alex and Tom flew into Yanji airport in Northern China, where they arrived at an airport *bulgogi* restaurant early for the one p.m. appointment with Abi and Harry. They found a table, ordered tea and biscuits, and worked on plans for the evening.

As they spoke, Tom received a text message from Langley that he read out loud. "Luke tracked to a location two miles east of Chongsong. Analysts suspect that Luke plans to cross the Tumen River tonight after dark about two kilometers north of the city."

"Can we assume that Luke has found a map?" Alex asked. "Border guards and local police on both sides of the border are likely to have that area under observation."

Tom slowly shook his head. "I'm not so sure. Smuggling is almost impossible in North Korea without bribing officials. The path of least resistance is more likely south of Chongsong, where local Chinese roads across the river are better. Harry can perhaps offer some insight regarding smuggling routes."

Alex looked up and noticed that Abi and Harry had entered the restaurant. She waved them over and invited them to sit down. Harry sat down, while Abi paced in front of the table. "How was your flight from Seoul?"

"Is there any news about Luke?" Abi said, ignoring the question. "I'm so worried about him that I can't concentrate."

"Actually, we don't expect news. Communication is heavily managed by the North Korean government. Their telephones, even cell phones, can't reach phones outside the country. Even simple things like electrical power aren't simple: The country shuts down at night for lack of electrical power," Tom said. "Harry, can you give us an update on smuggling routes and activities?"

"Sure. I heard that North Korean smugglers are excited about Party Foundation Day preparations, especially because of the free food involved. Local officials have been told to drop everything this week and next to organize celebrations. It seems odd because this year isn't a special anniversary, like the eightieth celebration a few years back. With officials busy, smuggling has stepped up. A lot of crossings are expected, starting tonight."

"If I were in North Korea and heard about all this excitement, I would take advantage of it," Tom said.

"Perhaps," Harry said, "but without some assistance, Luke would already be in custody. The North Koreans routinely set up roadblocks around cities and towns. Movement within the country is highly restricted. Local jurisdictions treat transit papers as conditioned on getting their share of the bribes."

Nodding, Tom said, "Luke's text—the head fake—earlier this week suggests that he has been getting assistance. Can we be ready to monitor crossings this evening?"

Harry looked up. "Yes. Local authorities will give us a two-ton truck and an army escort later this afternoon. What do I tell them about why a medical mission needs night vision goggles? Bootleg night vision goggles are a hot item, even for the People's Liberation Army."

Tom smiled. "The rumor is that hepatitis is being spread by North Korean refugees crossing over from

Chongsong,"

"Good story. One way or another, if we're going to observe smugglers in action tonight, we'll need to walk unobserved into the Tumen River basin before dark and take cover. There is no way of knowing who might show up."

§

The ridge t-boned the Tumen River just north of Chongsong leaving a narrow river valley before preceding to fork south and east on the Chinese side of the river. Chongsong itself lay at the foot of the ridge, built only slightly above an alluvial plain. The river snaked north through the plain past the village toward the ridge divide.

At 5:30 p.m., Ruth watched from their hillside perch while the ambulance with the three nurses made its way down the road to Chongsong Hospital and fog rose from the Tumen River to engulf the city and other low-lying areas, reducing visibility. After sunset, she led Luke in the moonlight around Chongsong just below the ridge-line and down the hill to the fog-covered road along the Tumen River, where the increasing glow of fireflies signaled the water's proximity. In the fog, she saw that she could see no more than thirty feet off, like the outline of other occasional workers walking or biking home to Shangbailong village further down the road. No one paid them any attention.

Ruth led Luke to where the river narrowed. There she left the road and found a large stone on the hill sheltered by a few bushes and trees where they could rest and observe everything. She invited Luke to sit on it. Then, a breeze came up and dissipated the fog. From this vantage point with the moonlight, she could see the road, the river, and the opposite shore. It was about nine-thirty in the evening.

"It looks easy to cross the river here," Luke whispered.

"Perhaps, but I suspect that during the day lookouts on the ridge over Chongsong can see this entire valley, including those Chinese villages opposite Chongsong that we saw earlier. With this moonlight, the military snipers may have been encouraged to work late." Ruth said.

"Now that you mentioned it, the Chinese shore opposite us is narrow and, unless you want to climb those hills, you must retreat south on the Chinese side right past Chongsong, making your escape obvious. Chinese border guards need only wait for you to pass their checkpoints in those villages opposite Chongsong that we saw earlier," Luke said.

At ten o'clock, a noisy, open-bed truck drove out of Chongsong and turned north on the road with its headlights shining up and down as it bounced along. When it got closer, it stopped. The driver and a local policeman got out, and they helped women climb off the back of the truck. Some got off themselves; others were tied up and needed assistance. Once they were all off the truck, the driver directed them with a flashlight towards the river. In the moonlight, Ruth recognized the three nurses from the park among those tied up. Some women fussed and cried; others just walked along looking down to avoid stumbling.

Ruth strained her eyes, covered her mouth, and grabbed Luke's hand tightly, working hard not to make a sound. *I wish that I had worked harder to convince those girls to avoid Chongsong Hospital.*

Another truck drove up on the Chinese side and stopped opposite the first; a uniformed man with a flashlight got out. The women waded the fifty meters across the river, while the man directed them towards the truck. A second man with a bamboo cane watched and prodded reluctant women, hitting them on the back. Once the truck was loaded and the women seated, it departed.

§

Electric pain radiated through Ruth's veins as fear burned inside her. Even as her mind began to leave her, she looked up and prayed, "Lord, help me."

Immediately, she heard crashing on the ridge line opposite her. She saw two glowing forms bounding down the hill, knocking down trees as they advanced towards the river. Once down the hill, they appeared in the open and sat like two panting, horse-sized Doberman pinchers, radiating like fireflies to light up and guard the Chinese beach. "Fear not," they said in unison.

Haechi angels! Ruth said to herself.

Ruth's pain and fear dissipated and the forms disappeared from sight. Ruth turned to Luke only to realize that she alone observed the spectacle of the beasts.

§

"I could have been one of those women tonight." Ruth said. "Does this sort of thing happen in America?"

"The short answer is yes. In the United States, human trafficking takes place mostly in the shadows among recent immigrants, the poor, the vulnerable, and drug addicts. Victims frequently suffer multiple afflictions, often including a history of abuse, abandonment, and psychiatric illness. Their abusers manipulate them, not just with sticks, but also with shame, guilt, and drugs."

As the trucks drove off, Ruth loosened her grip as her self-confident persona returned. She then turned to Luke. "Now it's our turn. Only we need to climb over those hills on the Chinese side."

Ruth led Luke down the hill and waded across the Tumen River hand-in-hand in the dark illuminated only by moonlight. As they approached the hill on the other side, a flashlight illuminated their faces.

Ruth and Luke froze.

"Luke, over here," Abi shouted and waved as she ran towards him.

"Abi? Oh, my goodness, what are you doing here?" Luke exclaimed and glanced at Ruth, letting go of her hand.

Reaching Luke, Abi threw her arms around him. "You're alive. After your plane crashed, I thought you were dead." Caught unaware, Luke stood there shocked and embarrassed, as Abi was fashionably dressed like a debutant on an evening picnic. He worried that Abi could smell his sweaty shirt that attracted so many unseen gnats in the night air.

Chapter Eleven

Standing on the shore of the Tumen River in China with his arms around Abi with Ruth still at his side, Luke realized that the flashlight illuminated Tom, Alex, Harry, and a contingent of Chinese soldiers with night goggles.

"Luke, what is going on? Who are these people?" Ruth whispered.

Abi let go of Luke and stepped back from Ruth, who stood as tall as Luke and made Abi look short. "Luke, who, who is this woman?"

Luke paused and extended his arm toward Ruth. "Abi, this is Ruth. Her father pulled me out of the Sea of Japan semiconscious in the middle of the recent typhoon. Ruth guided me out of North Korea, risking her life and freedom to bring me here."

Abi glared at Ruth with piercing eyes, oblivious to what had just been said. Even in the dark without make-up, and dressed in worker's clothes, Ruth's stunning appearance evoked a visceral reaction in Abi.

Luke ignored Abi's rage and turned to Ruth. "Ruth, this is my fiancé, Abi. The man with the flashlight is Harry from Beijing; next to him are Tom and Alex from Virginia. I do not know the men in uniform who are standing with them."

One of the soldiers behind Abi pulled off his night goggles and stepped to the side. "North Korean guards have orders to shoot those crossing the border on sight. How convenient," Lei Han said as he chambered a round in his AK-47.

Floodlights from the North Korean side of the river illuminated everyone.

"Drop your weapons. Hold your hands up where I can see them," a commanding voice ordered by bull-horn.

Luke wondered how he had missed the presence of a searchlight and a detachment of soldiers so close to where Ruth and he had been sitting. *Were these soldiers North Korean commandos schooled in camouflage? No. The stylish uniforms and open door to an underground bunker suggested that border guards kept a close watch on this stretch of the Tumen.*

Lei Han shouted back, "Who are you? This is Chinese sovereign territory. You have no jurisdiction here."

"I'm Mr. Parks, Director of the Reconnaissance General Bureau. I'm authorized to assist the Director of the Chinese State Security agency in apprehending any rogue elements. Isn't that true, Harry?"

"That's right, Mr. Parks," Harry responded.

"Lei Han, you're accused of perpetrating counter-revolutionary activities by sabotaging a commercial airline over the air space of the Democratic People's Republic of Korea. Give up your weapon; you're under arrest," Mr. Parks demanded.

"You have no proof. Besides, I acted in the best interests of both our countries," Lei Han yelled back.

Lei Han began to shake violently, dropped his gun, and clutched his chest before dropping to his knees with his head bowed.

Harry called out, "Lei Han is having a nervous breakdown."

Abi screamed, "Lei Han." She ran over, kneeled

beside him, and took his hand. "I told you to stop pursuing me."

Lei Han looked up and whispered, "I love you."

Abi threw her arms around him and cried, "You silly man."

Harry walked over and confiscated Lei Han's AK-47 and said, "Lei Han, you're under arrest under the authority of the Ministry of State Security for sedition against the government of the People's Republic of China."

Mr. Parks wadded across the Tumen River and shook Harry's hand. "Harry, I'll let you take care of the prisoner." He smiled. "I apologize for all the drama. It is important to our Supreme Leader that these lovebirds get back together and Chinese-American relations continue to improve, but this policy is strictly confidential. It is best for the media to believe that Luke escaped from North Korea by himself with the assistance of the dashing young woman, Ruth Chŭ."

Mr. Parks turned to Tom and shook his hand. "Tom, I don't think that we have been formally introduced. We're in the same business, just with different companies. Perhaps, we'll meet again under more favorable circumstances."

Mr. Parks turned and waded back across the Tumen River into North Korea.

The floodlights went dark. Abi and a soldier helped Lei Han walk back to the vehicles.

"Who will feed Mr. Premier? Promise me that you will feed him." Lei Han mumbled with head still bowed.

The rest of the group followed behind.

Chapter Twelve

*A*fter returning to Beijing, Abi broke off her engagement with Luke and lobbied her father to have the Chinese Communist Party pardon Lei Han, who nevertheless disappeared from public view. Unsure of herself, bothered by her arrogance, and ashamed of the pain she caused so many people, Abi remained in Beijing out of the public eye for Christmas, spent January at a mountain retreat in North Carolina, and later reluctantly returned to Baltimore for the spring semester to continue her medical studies.

Ruth flew back to Washington Dulles International Airport with Tom, Alex, and Luke, where she was met at the airport by her uncle, Pastor Chǔ, and most of his church's congregation. Airport security turned out in force to manage the strong media presence anxious to hear about Luke's escape from North Korea and to get a glimpse of the mysterious woman who engineered his escape.

The following week Pastor Chǔ's congregation hosted a church-wide dinner in Ruth's honor that Tom,

Alex, and Luke attended. Harry also showed up and spent time talking with Tom over dinner. Luke and Alex sat with Ruth and her uncle, smiling and laughing.

The vice president also appeared at the event to honor Ruth in helping Luke leave North Korea and shared dinner with a presumed member of the congregation, a Mr. Parks. The media presence at a North Korean congregational gathering drew attention to the plight of North Koreans during sanctions, especially those working in the fisheries industry and women being trafficked into China.

When journalists asked the vice president about sanctions on North Korea, he said that the Administration planned a policy review in the coming weeks in cooperation with Chinese and South Korean allies. During the vice president's presentation and the interviews that followed, Mr. Parks stood off to the side with his hands folded, said nothing, and smiled.

When newscasters asked Luke about Sarah, he responded, "Sarah was buried at sea, but we plan to hold a remembrance service to honor her life. Later, we will commission a headstone and place it in the family burial plot behind the church." The balance that Luke sought in his life returned with his new responsibilities and he found peace in the consolation that he had reconciled with Sarah before she died.

In the months that followed, several members of Luke's congregation claimed to have seen someone who looked like him at different times and places in Georgetown in the company of the dashing young Asian law student. However, that fellow looked altogether younger and more self-assured than the placid pastor that they had grown accustomed to.

ABOUT

*A*uthor Stephen W. Hiemstra lives in Centreville, Virginia, with Maryam, his wife of more than thirty-five years. They have three grown children.

Stephen worked as an economist for twenty-seven years in more than five federal agencies, where he published numerous government studies, magazine articles, and book reviews. Check WorldCat.org for a complete listing of volumes available in a library near you.

He wrote his first book, *A Christian Guide to Spirituality* in 2014. In 2015, he translated and published a Spanish edition, *Una Guía Cristiana a la Espiritualidad*. In 2016, he wrote a second book, *Life in Tension*, which also focuses on Christian spirituality. A Spanish edition appeared in 2021—*Vida en Tensión*. In 2017, he published a memoir, *Called Along the Way*. In 2018, he published a *Spiritual Trilogy* (an eBook compilation) and his first hardcover book, *Everyday Prayers for Everyday People*. In 2019, he published *Simple Faith*. In 2020, he published *Living in Christ*, which is the fifth book in his Christian spirituality series. In 2021, he published his debut novella, *Masquerade*, and rewrote it as a screenplay under the title: *Brandishing the Blue*. In 2022, he translated and published his first book in German: *Ein Christlicher Leitfaden zur Spiritualität*. In early 2023, he published the sixth book in his series, *Image and Illumination*, and published the first book in a new series, *The Image of God in the Parables*.

Stephen has a Masters of Divinity (MDiv, 2013) from Gordon-Conwell Theological Seminary in Charlotte, North Carolina. His doctorate (Ph.D., 1985) is in agricultural economics from Michigan State University. He studied in Puerto Rico and in Germany, and speaks Spanish and German.

Correspond with Stephen at T2Pneuma@gmail.com or follow his blog at http://www.T2Pneuma.net.

If you enjoyed *The Detour*, please post a review online.